THE WORLD HE ONCE KNEW

MICAH CASTLE

The World He Once Knew

Micah Castle

Fedowar Press, LLC

www.FedowarPress.com

ISBN-13 (Digital): 978-1-956492-48-4
ISBN-13 (Paperback): 978-1-956492-49-1

Edited by Heather Ann Larson
Cover Art by Don Noble of Rooster Republic Press
Interior Design by D.W. Hitz

THE WORLD HE ONCE KNEW is a work of fiction. Names, characters, places, and incidents are either products of the author's imagination, or the authors have used them fictitiously. Any resemblance to actual events or persons, living or dead, is entirely coincidental.

CONTENT WARNINGS are available at the end of this book. Please consult this list for any particular subject matter you may be sensitive to.

Also By Micah Castle

Reconstructing A Relationship (D&T Publishing)
The Abyss Beyond the Reflection

To my beautiful wife, Nikki, who without her this book wouldn't have been written.

The World He Once Knew

F RIGID AIR EJECTS FROM his lungs when the electricity floods his body. Stinging eyes wide open, a wall towers over him, a bay of light blue and white hexagonal protrusions extending into the dark recesses hiding the ceiling. He coughs and hacks, doubling over, covering his mouth with his fist.

"He all right?" someone says from behind him.

"Ya, always happens to 'em when they first come to," a harsh, different voice says.

He opens his eyes once his breathing settles. He realizes he's nude, on a metal bed. An opening, opaque with cold, billowing mist, is beyond his pale feet. Silhouetted, dangling wires can be made out, some with transparent pads at their ends.

No, wait... I'm not naked, this person is.

This isn't me.

This isn't my body.

He moves his hand into view. It moves the way he wants and how he tells it to, but it isn't the hand he knows. He can't remember why it's different, a point of reference gone, unobtainable. Gripping the fat of the hairy thigh, he probes muscle and bone. He feels it, yet it's not the same somehow.

His head begins pounding.

"Can ya hurry the hell up?" someone says. "We got people waiting."

A hand slaps his upper back, and a short man with a beak

nose, widely-spaced, beady eyes, and a ring of tousled hair surrounding a scarred scalp leans to his side. "Hey. I know it's a lot to process, but we're holding up the line." He slides his hand off and turns away. "C'mon, I'll explain it all over sup."

He rubs the back of his head, finding short hair but no exit wound nor scar. He's unsure why he expects to find those in the first place. He glances over his shoulder. A giant, greasy man with a bulging gut and wearing rounded sunglasses stands by some type of computer system, near an empty doorway. The monitor's blue light gives his sweat sheen. The short man is off to the side, his hands in his washed-out, blue jumpsuit pockets, his forearms thick with dark hair.

"You coming or what, Jay?" Short Man says.

Giant Man groans, rubs his nose across his hairless arm. "Asshole, hurry it up."

He can't recall if his name's Jay or not, but it must be for the Short Man to call him that.

Jay slowly turns on the metal bed, his legs dangling. Even slower, he slips down onto the cold, hard floor. Vertigo washes over him momentarily then clears. It takes Jay a bit to remember how to walk, how hips and legs and feet are meant to be used. Luckily, Short Man holds his arm, and he uses his shoulder for support.

Through the doorway, another door reveals a low-ceilinged room congested with people sitting and standing, but Short Man guides Jay down a narrow, dimly lit hall.

"Next!" the Fat Man shouts.

Jay's led into a small room, more of a closet, with a hole in the ground under a rusted faucet and broken mirror.

"Ignore those," Short Man says and points to the corner where clothes have been thrown carelessly. "There's your suit, boots are under them. Put 'em on and we'll get out of this shithole."

The scratchy material irritates Jay's skin as he steps into the legs, slides his arms through, and zips the front. The boots mold to his feet and aren't so bad. His genitals don't agree with the suit, unable to find comfort.

"Jewels giving you problems?"

Jay looks from his groin to him. Nods.

"Happens to everyone. You'll get used to it."

He gives another futile adjustment as he's ushered back into the hall. Going the opposite way of where Giant Man is, descending a short flight of stairs and through a battered door with a busted EXIT sign above it, they come out to...

"Jesus," he mutters with a voice deeper than his own.

Dark walls rise into the black sky in front of and behind him. Mustard yellow litter piles against the bottom. Some parts of the buildings are covered in unfamiliar symbols and lettering in glowing green and blue graffiti; others are plastered under layers of frayed posters, weathered to the point that their information and sigils are indecipherable. In the sky, tiny white lights drift past, like he's at the bottom of a lake looking up at passing boats.

Jay is pulled by the man but can't help to keep staring above. Other lights appear: red, green, and yellow, spaced out in ovals or rounded rectangles among white dots, strobing and pulsing like airplanes in the night. Beyond, further above, is a smooth, curved surface. So faint Jay hardly recognizes it in the light pollution. It reminds him of a dome.

"Hey." Short Man pulls down Jay's face by his chin. "Look at me." The man casts a short shadow standing in the foggy light that falls into the alley. "I know there's a lot to take in. I get it. But we're not dicking around while you're on the clock."

"On the clock?"

"Uh huh," he says. "Why do you think you're here? For vaca?"

Jay's brain feels like mush when he tries to remember before here, before waking up in the cold room, only recalling incomplete snapshots of houses and roads and buildings, food and drinks, other random bits. Like rifling through a box full of knickknacks left from bygone owners.

"Uh..."

Short Man rolls his eyes, turns around. "Fucking HUSKs, I swear..." He waves his hand. "Just follow me. Keep your eyes low, hands in your pockets. You'll have time to blow after we're done."

Their travel is short-lived. They take a right onto a narrow street overcrowded with signs and shopfronts and multicolored LEDs in the shape of weird letters Jay can't read. People meander past or huddle in groups alongside shops. A collection of gray smog hovers above. Short Man opens a frosted door, stomps down uneven stairs and goes through another door, Jay in tow.

Inside is even more suffocating. There are no windows and only one other door in the back. Side-by-side booths along the walls brim with pale people eating and drinking from beige bowls; some are only smoking needle-thin sticks. They're wearing the same outfit as Jay. Some have cut off the legs or arms, and a few have removed or pulled down the top, revealing chests and shoulder tattoos in dark and white ink. A mishmash of symbols and illustrations, but one is redundant: a hollow circle with a silhouette raindrop in the center.

Incoherent chitter-chatter swells against the low ceiling, and smoke clogs the recessed lighting. Jay can't hear Short Man speaking. He follows him across the linoleum to a booth in the back. Eyes—some normal, others dimly illuminated by lines of light blue, green, or white—follow them, but Jay keeps his vision down.

Short Man slides into one side and tells Jay to take the other.

It looks soft, but it's hard against his ass.

A flatscreen monitor's flush with the wall. Short Man leans over the orange-brown table and presses a button along the screen's bottom. The air becomes electrified, and the outside noise immediately quiets. Dead silence. It's not heavy or palpable, just vacant of sound.

"That's better," he mutters, pressing more icons that flash by in technicolor. The screen turns white with two red letters: *TY*.

"What's—" Jay starts.

"Food first," Short Man shushes him.

A section of the wall opens beneath the monitor, and a yellow bowl slides out with a bundle of matching utensils. Short Man snatches both, bringing them close. He undoes the bundle, letting chopsticks and a spoon fall where they may, and uses a fork to slurp purple noodles from the bowl.

"Ahhh," he sighs, finishing it fast. Jay leans in, preparing to talk again, but then Short Man eats the bowl and utensils, even the tie that bundled them together. They crunch like chips.

"Okay, okay," Jay spits. "What's going on? What year is it? Who are you? Where are we?"

Short Man wipes his lips, an oil trail left on his hand. "It's 2792. Name's Rey Crews, just call me Crews. You're on the Moon, if you remember it from back when."

Jay feels like his mind should be reeling, but it's like what Crews says is validating what he already knew, though he's certain he never learned it. "And the place I woke up in? This place? Out there?"

"HUSK storage; Z'teehs, food chain everywhere in this side of town; back market in Elusk-DS5."

"What's a husk? You said that before."

"H.U.S.K. Humanoid Upload something something..." Crews waves his hand in front of his face. "I don't remember the rest, and it really doesn't matter. Basically, you're a digital copy of yourself in a body that's kinda human, kinda not."

"A digital copy?" he says.

"Yup. Hella cheap, too. Gotta love your RFD."

Jay runs an unfamiliar hand over his unfamiliar face, expecting sweat, but his skin's dry.

Jesus Christ...

His thoughts spin as though trapped in a tornado, sense and logic thrown violently against every known surface, attempting to grab onto something—anything—to ground him.

"Uh..."

Crews sighs. "Guess they don't preload that info on the cheap... Wonder what else wasn't included," he mutters, rubbing his rounded chin. "They better not have..." He sets his meaty elbows on the table. "Look, it's really nothing to freak about. You died a long time ago, and so has everyone else you knew. Now you're here, alive, mostly, and well. Just your original body with the brain and other giblets, *clearly*, isn't around anymore." Crews snickers. "Hell, not even on this planet—"

"From what?"

"What?"

"Died. How'd I die?"

"You don't know that either?"

Jay shakes his head.

"Making me do *all* the work, huh? Your reason for departure was suicide." He makes his hand into a gun, shoves his finger into his mouth, and his thumb depresses. Cocks his head back. "Reasoning unknown, though. No note or will, if I remember right. Likely from work, though. You were a detective—probably seen some shit you couldn't handle, or I don't fucking know."

"Why would I do that?" Jay says, struggling through nothing-ness for a reason why he would've killed himself, yet there are no memories leading up to or of it... A blank slate. An abyss. "I was a detective..."

"Uh huh, that's why you were picked, besides the low price. You also had a family, I think, and a sister maybe."

"Why would you need a detective?" *A family? I had one? No, wait, yes: Nicole, my wife; Ashleigh, my sister.* No memories or images appear in his mind, only first names... *But why does it feel like I care more about finding out I was a detective than my own family?*

He rubs his calloused hands together. "I needed someone who knows what they're doing. From your data, you weren't the best, but you were capable."

"People can pay to bring people back from the dead to *work?*"

"A copy. People can pay for a *digital copy* to be *uploaded* into a HUSK. Originals are disgustingly expensive, not taking into account their bodies. Only the most wealthy folks are kept unique. On ice somewhere on Europa."

Jay rubs his eyes. "Okay, fine, whatever, but what if I don't want to work? What if I decide to run off?"

He laughs. "You'll be terminated for breaching the buyer/seller contract and exported back into the digital banks. The lifeless HUSK will be found wherever it dropped and repurposed or destroyed."

Again, Jay feels like he should be losing his mind, but it's like talking about the weather, what he had for supper. Normal. Everyday. Routine.

My palms should be clammy, my temples pounding; I should be losing my shit, going fucking insane about being brought back to life, being on the Moon, being a digital version of myself, of learning about my own apparent suicide; of so many other questions and things springing from this well of unimaginable information. Yet I'm cool, collected, calm. Like I already knew all this before in a past I don't have or can't remember. Is it a part of the HUSK thing too? Did they alter my... code—*I guess?—so I wouldn't go ballistic, wouldn't crumble under the impossible weight of being thrown headfirst into the distant future?*

"A lot to take in," Crews says. "I know. But we got shit to do, so I'll allow ya one more question for now, before we get down to brass tax."

"Uh..." Jay searches for something worthwhile to ask but fails. "What happened to Earth?"

"It's there—worse for wear, but there. People still live there, even after the shit they put it through. Even with all the real estate here and on Mars, I don't blame them. Nothing so far holds a candle to Earth, at least in its prime."

Jay nods like he knows what he's on about. "Uh huh..."

Crews claps his hands together. "Okay, so." His fingers intertwine and point at Jay. "You were HUSK'd because I need someone to figure out what happened to one of my ships, the *Candlewood*."

"Spaceship, you mean, right?"

"No shit.

"It's a transporter. Picks up shipments and takes them somewhere else—food, supplies, tools, etc. Whatever can be fitted into a container, we move it no questions asked. Anyway, it went dark fourteen days ago. No response from any of the crew, and it looks like its power's down too. Took a while to scrounge up the money for you and a renter, but we're good now."

"So, you need me to figure out what happened? How would I do that?"

"For a detective, you're fuckin' stupid. You're going to get on the ship, Jay. I'll be near, in the renter, and we'll talk through short-wave. Though to be frank, I'm no pilot, but we shouldn't have any problems getting there and back. Ship drives itself mostly anyway."

"Okay..." Jay says. "But why don't you just call the police or someone to handle it? They still exist, right?"

"I don't want them sticking their snouts into my business. Let's say not everything we carry is... What was the word? *Kosher*."

"And... am I getting paid or something for this? Is money still around?"

"Of course it is!" Crews slaps the table. "How do you think life would be without money? It's all digital now, though, chipped into your HUSK wrist by whatever company's sponsoring the facility at the time. Don't even need a PIN. But yeah, you're getting paid. Half now, half after."

"How much?"

"Fifty-K now, then 50K after."

Jay's eyes widen. "Fifty-thousand dollars?"

"Don't get too giddy. The value of money went down the shitter over the millennia." He scratches his stubbled cheek, looking away. "If my math's right—probably isn't—but 50K in yester-year's money is probably around $500."

"Oh..."

"Yup. So, anyway. We leave pronto."

"Already?"

"Time is money and I ain't wasting it on you."

Jay hesitates but slides out of the booth.

The gibbering chatter of the other people bombards him. Some watch him as he and Crews beeline to the exit, and they have to step aside for two short women holding hands coming down the stairs. Outside, the narrow street is less congested than before but still cluttered.

Giant signs jut from buildings and shop fronts with neon and

LED letters that look like English but also Chinese and a little Spanish. Varying crude symbols of what must be company logos plaster most of the flickering billboards looming overhead. The circle with the raindrop is stenciled on some of the surfaces in red paint. *Is it a club or something? A gang? I remember gang symbols graffitied on overpasses... Is that still going on? Thought we'd be past all those stupid squabbles by the time we accomplished living on other planets.*

"So, another thing that may help you," Crews says over the chattering din. "HUSKs are equipped with the goods, as you already know, but their function isn't mandatory. Meaning you can use it or not, like normal people. But what isn't functional is most of your insides, which you don't really have. I mean, they're *there* but for decoration. So, you don't get hungry or thirsty, you can't eat or drink, and you can't shit, piss, cry, sweat, smell, taste, etc."

At the end of the street are tall, tightly packed buildings, and in the distance, Jay can make out a towering gray wall. *A skyscraper?* "I can have sex?" he says, glancing over his shoulder. The opposite end is the same sans the wall.

"If ya want, yeah. Don't ask me why they made them that way,probably a male engineer thought it was a great idea. And I can't say I disagree—it's just the way HUSKs are. The more expensive models have the luxury of taste buds and/or the ability to smell, even not feel pain, but who has money to waste for that?"

Sidestepping folks who ogle him like Jay's interesting or hideous, they pass a manhole blocked off by short, yel-low-and-white barriers. He peeks to find a ladder and a mess of black wiring descending into gloom. "But I still need air and a heart? Sounds ass-backwards." Then he notices there are no telephone posts or wires hanging above... *Ah, they run through the ground now.*

Everyone's dressed in the same or similar jumpsuit, though altered here and there, same as the restaurant. The circle-rain-drop emblem appears sporadically, while what must be the opposite tattoo does too: a circle filled in black, a raindrop hovering above it.

The rival gang? None seem to be hostile. Not watching each other, not avoiding one another, no one's bothering anyone. Hell, I can't even see any weapons... Doesn't mean they're not there.

Jay can't stop his growing curiosity. He feels the pull of investigating, of wanting to learn what's going on, the gears and bolts of the place. He wants to figure out who's the 'bad guys,' 'good guys,' the ones to look out for, the ones he could ask for help if he needed it...

"Cheaper to repurpose and augment some saps lungs and heart than make batteries tiny enough to fit into a human body that'll last long enough to matter." Crews waves a hand in front of his face.

He barely listens to Crews as he pushes down his detective brain. He figures he'll be able to scratch that itch later. He focuses on the frosted window displays and shopfronts. Bars and clubs with tinted windows, some dimly lit with strobing illuminance breathing in dark fog in sync with music he can feel outside. Eateries every three or so stops, all similar to Z'teehs—if not the same: tiny sections sterilely lit, an enormous amount of foil wrapped food spilling over metal shelving. No workers anywhere, just customers eating in booths, leaning against counters, sitting on stools, grabbing things from shelves; no one buying anything with cards or PIN pads or cash, every-thing amazingly automatic, seamless.

Shops and crowds give way to quiet, tall buildings with rows of narrow windows, spreading to heights Jay can't see without craning his head back the farthest it'll go. Small flights of steps lead to dirty double doors; some folks sit out on the stoops. It's the first time he's seen children so far. They wear the same style of clothes, albeit smaller, and sit by or on the knees of their apparent parents, who leisurely chat to one another about things Jay can't hear. Some have open tins of steaming drinks. Jay wonders—if he could smell, would it smell like the bitter aroma of coffee or the soothing scents of tea.

These people vaguely remind him of the working class of his own era. Single fathers, mothers; parents spending what little time they had at the end of the day, despite being exhausted from little pay and long shifts, with their loved ones before going to bed to start the cycle again. It feels like the end of summer, and he wishes there was a sky ablaze with the dying sun alighting the dim area...

A tall man with hands in his pockets shoulders Jay, spitting under his breath: "Fucking HUSK."

Jay rights himself before falling and says to Crews: "How'd he know I'm a HUSK?"

Pavement spreads like water into a circular park surrounded by trees—*oak? Can't be*—missing chunks of leaves sprouting from unkempt grass. A rusted bench sits before a murky pool with a fountain in the center that doesn't spray.

They stop by the bench and Crews sits with a sigh. "I need to take a break, but it's your eyes, buddy. You got those weird HUSK eyes."

He plods to the lake and catches a glimpse of his reflection in a patch free of murk.

Shit.

His eyes are different, *way* different. There is a rounded, white-blue crosshair superimposed over his brown irises, a dot of the same color in the center of his black pupils, and clear scleras, no veins to be seen. But his face looks plain, boring, no defining characteristics. Average chin, nose, ears not too small or too big, eyes spaced apart well enough, brown eyebrows and short hair, and what he considers normal-sized lips. He can't recollect what his face looked like before, so with no comparison Jay takes in his reflection with ease.

If it weren't for the HUSK eyes, no one could pick me out of the crowd. An Average Joe.

Turning away, he leaves Crews to rest and goes to a tree. Jay discovers it's fake; what leaves remain are made from scratchy, cloth material, its bark like sandpaper. Breaking a leaf apart, gray powder spills out. *Wonder if they smell like real trees?*

He waves his boot through the grass before crouching. He plucks a blade from the ground, and it feels the same as the tree.

Glancing toward the opposite end of the park, he finds it leads into another section of quiet complexes. Beyond, the giant, gray wall looms over everything, the dome keeping immediate death away from the city curves, further in, down behind the wall. Picturing the city from above, he imagines it looks like a bundt cake.

He looks up and tiny lights flicker past in the empty nothing and the subtle sheen of the dome; there are faint stars.

Can't see Earth... No Sun, either... Must be on the dark side.

A sense of longing and loss ebbs through him though it's been hundreds of years since he was home. He tries to recall regular things besides his job—walking down the street, picking up a coffee from a café, what his car looked like, what his house looked like, what his home life was like—he knows his wife's and sister's names but nothing more.

Still insane, I'm here and alive in the far future. I'm on the damn Moon living in a biodome.

Questions he wishes to ask but not wanting to bother Crews about swell in his mind: Is there somewhere I can read about the past, somewhere I can find if the people I knew were uploaded in the future too? Who first colonized the Moon? What exactly led to Earth's downfall, and how're people surviving now? And what about Mars? How is it there compared to here?

A couple meanders past with their daughter between them, all hand in hand. The adults are both bald, the hollow circle with the center raindrop on the nape of their necks, their child with a mop of pale blonde hair down to her shoulders. She glances at him, her wide eyes streaked with glowing white lines, then looks ahead.

Wonder if the person inside that little girl is her or someone else... How does that work? Is she going to get older or is her body going to stay the same while her psyche ages? That would suck.

His thoughts transition: *I still don't know what the hell that tattoo means.*

Crews stands, slapping his knees. "Alright, if you're done fuckin' around, let's get out of here."

Jay catches up with him. "What do the tattoos mean?"

"Ah..." He glances around. "Rather get into that when we're on the ship."

"Okay."

They follow the road through the close-knit, quiet buildings. It must be early for only a handful of folks are out, sipping from steaming tins. Small, weakly lit orbs flank the street, providing enough illuminance to see by. Without the sun, he has no idea if it's morning or not.

The road splits. Ahead, the neighborhood appears to improve; buildings are less crowded, sturdier, cleaner; streets are wider, newer looking, more and brighter light orbs along the side; and the giant wall in the distance makes him wonder what's behind it. They take a left, slowing as the road begins to slope downwards.

Complexes and lights lessen, replaced by single-story homes packed together, sterile lights casting from towering light posts of what must be the ship bay. Clatter and clunking and whining of metal floods his ears. Four jutting docks, unevenly spaced, hang over emptiness; two are vacant.

A weathered, windowless ship, seemingly patched together with scrap metal, is parked in one, and a top-heavy vessel with a hexagonal protrusion hanging over its downward-slanting front is docked in the other. People in orange jumpsuits, neon green hardhats, and holographic visors move from broken ships to stations with cranes, machinery, and workbenches with welding torches. Sparks spray as workers hunch over metallic material with electric hand saws. An enormous, gray structure with rows of slats along its sides nearly touches the dome in the far back.

That must be the garage.

They reach the bottom of the hill. Pavement gives way to metal; footsteps clank. They hurry past the workers, who pay them no mind, and make for the discolored ship. It looms over him, its hull resting atop small, rusted rails, and its rear, trapezoid thrusters rest on the edge of the bay. To Jay, they seem enormous for the ship, kind of lopsided. The sleek, black windshield covers the entire narrow front.

Crews says, "I'm home," and the section of the side facing them depresses, slides to the left, and a bridge glides out, stopping at the dock.

"Let's get this ball rolling." He waves Jay onto the ship.

———————

Inside, it's cramped like an RV. An aisle runs from the front to the rear, veering to the right. A small table and two chairs that fold up are bolted to the wall; cold storage is on the opposite side, filled with reflective packets of what Crews tells Jay are dehydrated food and hydration packs—"You won't be needing any of those." He leads him down the hall.

"So," he asks again the second they're on the ship, "what's with those tattoos people have?"

"Which ones?"

They stop before a transparent barrier blocking the remainder of the ship. There's a thin door inlaid into the wall to their right. Beyond is a white room, sterilely lit, and a sealed door flush to the far wall.

"Looks like a circle with a little raindrop in its center. Saw another one, too, but the circle was full and the raindrop was above it. Are they gangs or something?"

"Something," Crews says. "Some folks aren't happy with the way things are going; others are."

"How?"

Crews sighs. "People believe that things ought to return to the way they were, to humanity's roots and all that. Kind of like... What were those people called in your day? Hip..."

"Hippies?"

"Yeah, that." He nods. "Like them. Nature and trees and all that bullshit. They believe leaving the Earth is a big no-go, but not much of a choice when it's gone to shit, huh?"

"And the other tattoo? Is that their enemy?"

"Kinda. They think the opposite, that humanity shouldn't be stuck to just one planet, should accept progress and advancements and yada, yada, yada."

"But they weren't fighting in town?" He throws a thumb over his shoulder.

"No shit. We're not *animals*, Jay. It's copacetic in towns, cities, etc., though underground warfare isn't unheard of."

"So what do you believe?"

Crews meets Jay's eyes. "I believe whoever's paying more in this civil war."

"Really?"

"Christ... People have fought over dumber shit, Jay. I might as well get something out of it." He grumbles. "Anyway, can I show you the rest of the ship or what?"

"Sorry, one more. What's with the big wall?"

"Segregation," he spits.

"That's happening again?" Jay says, wide-eyed.

"The powers that be don't call it that, but it's about wealth, not race. They won't say that either."

"Keep the rich in, poor out?"

Crews nods. "Uh huh. They say it's for 'protection of 05's power gridwork and security of the inner dome's structure,' but it's all bullshit." He runs a hand under his bulbous nose. "It's so they have control of everything, so the folks in power can leave lickity-split if shit goes south."

Silence.

"You done now?" Crews spits.

"I guess."

"Great." He points to the white room. "That's the airlock, but this is where you change into your suit." Crews presses the door; it splits and slides back. A single, sleek, apricot suit hangs from a hook. Thick, copper lines outlined by glossy black snake all over it.

"The helmet's in the airlock." He points toward the white room then closes the closet. "We'll suit you up once we make it to the *Candlewood*."

Jay steps aside as Crews shuffles past and plods to the front of the ship. The pilot bay has two belted, reclined seats before the curved, tinted windshields. Buttons and switches of varying colors cover the curved walls, the center console, and parts of the ceiling.

Crews falls into one, then pats the other for Jay to do the same. Crews flicks a switch overhead, and they listen to the grinding whine of the bridge being withdrawn. With a hiss and click, the door closes too.

"All right, I know this piss bucket doesn't look like much, but it's graded for longer travels than what we gotta do. And you might be wondering 'Where's the wheel?'—those aren't used much anymore. Everything's automatic now." He presses a purple button. Belts slide out from the chair and over them, tightening, digging into Jay's chest. "And you might also wonder 'But what if the system fails?' To that I'd say if the ship fails, even with a manual drive, we'd still be fucked. Remember, I'm not a pilot." Crews leans to the side, flicking another switch. "But to make this easier on you, I'll pump you with KOC first, then I'll go under once we're in a straight shot to the ship. This old Betty will handle the rest."

"KOC?" Jay says quietly.

"Knock Out Concoction. You'd think we'd have better names for things by now, but we care even less than they did in your time." He pulls a green lever, twists, and depresses it. Needles stab Jay's rear, his back, arms, legs, and the nape of his neck. He tries to leap out of his seat, but the belts keep him pinned.

"Don't fight it, Jay. It'll be fine," Crews says. "It's going to feel like... Like that stuff dentists used to use, so I've been told. That cool, comfortable feeling should be coming..."

Winter fills Jay's lungs. He exhales white mist. His heart freezes over. His nose and cheeks tingle, and his eyes gloss over as a smile crosses his face. Muscles relax, deflate, and he's melting into a puddle in his seat.

Crews chuckles. "Just be glad you're a HUSK. Don't have to get the tubes like I do." His flattened, deep, loud words contort... Jay tries to talk, but his lips are mushy rivulets, refusing to abide. He slowly slides down an icy shaft and plummets into a complete pitch more welcome than anything else in the world.

———

"You awake?

"Jay?

"The WUC should be kicking in..."

Jay gasps like he's coming up for air and his heart hammers against his chest. He lunges forward, reaching for something or someone, only to be wrenched back by the belts.

"What," he forces out between breaths, his tongue fuzzy, "Did you do—to me?"

"Relax," Crews says, his hands on his lap. He now has a patchy, wild mustache and beard, grown down his neck. "Deep breathes, everything's fine."

Jay listens, and minutes later, his lungs calm and his heart steadies. He runs a hand over his face to find it as smooth as before. HUSKs don't grow hair either. "Are we there?"

"Yup." Crews flips an overhead switch; the windshields flicker like screens then come to life with a picture of the *Candlewood*, illuminated by several floodlights. "There she blows."

It's similar to the ship they're in but on a much bigger scale: a squarish, gray hull with the inward slanting bottom, a pointed front, and four giant thrusters jutting from the rear. It's rusty and weathered, but Jay's unsure if it's from age or if it's like an old beat-up car; looks don't matter, it's only something to use to move things from A to B.

"There's a cargo bay on the other side," Crews says, coughing into his fist then continuing: "Big ol' fuckin' door... She looks about the same as she did when I last saw her."

"And when was that?" Jay asks, his tongue prickly.

"A year or two, maybe." He shrugs. "Since its last inspection at least."

Crews uncovers a blue button on the console and presses it. Their belts unhook and slither back underneath the chair.

Jay takes a deep breath, as though it's his first one in a long while. Before Jay can enjoy being awake or in outer space for the first time, Crews slides off his seat, zips up an opening on his groin and rear, and slaps Jay on the shoulder.

"C'mon, let's get you suited up."

"Legs first." Crews stands by as Jay, nude, stops from putting his arms in and begins pulling the bottom half up over his pale calves. "Then arms." The tight, silicon-like material shrinks against his skin as he manages to get all his limbs in the suit. His hands and feet poking out at the ends looks comical to him.

Crews turns him around and seals the front of the suit. There's no zipper or buttons, but some sort of magnetic strip that, when connected, makes it seem like the suit's entirely one piece.

"Looking sharp," he says, stepping back.

Jay glances over his body. It's like a second skin. A flurry of copper lines outlined in black cover him. He imagines they are like wires or conductors, something he could feel when wearing the suit, but he doesn't feel either of them. They run down his arms, over his chest, down his legs, and around his back to a wide, black line circling around his waist. Four small, empty cylindrical pockets are indented in his right flank.

"What's that for?"

Crews crouches in front of the closet. He reaches in and pulls out a pair of grayish purple boots, a line around the bottom similar to the suit Jay's already wearing. He sets them before Jay.

"The boots? Walking or running, if you're so inclined."

Jay shoves one foot in. It pressure-seals around his shin. He repeats the process with the other one. "No, the little pockets on my ass."

"Oh! Those are O2 holders."

In the boots, he's a few inches taller.

Can get used to this too...

"And what's the O2 in? Batteries?"

"Cartridges." Crews nods to the airlock. "They're in there, with the helmet and gloves."

"Gloves?"

"Yeah." Crews chuckles. "You think I'd send you into the unknown without at least some protection? They're like the boots—pressure sealed and airtight—but don't have mags."

"Mags?" Jay feels like a dumbass for asking all these questions.

"Short for magnets," Crews groans. "Once you have everything on, I'll explain how it all works." He moves to the translucent wall, puts his palm on it, and waves Jay over.

A door hisses open. Jay believes he should be afraid, should be filled with anticipation, anxiety, dread, *something*, but he's not. It's like being back at the restaurant: knowing without remembering how he knows; hereditary information, not learned.

The door seals behind him, Crews remaining on the other side. It's a tiny room with clear walls, and unseen openings in the corners whistle cold, pressurized air. The floor rumbles, rattling his fake innards. The whistling ceases, and another door opens into the airlock.

It's about the size of a one-car garage, empty save for a yellowed chest against the wall.

"You hear me?" Crews's voice issues from a speaker somewhere in the ceiling.

"Yeah," Jay says, glancing at the transparent barrier to find Crews gone.

"Good, wasn't sure this would work. Haven't tried it until now. Anyway, in the box is the helmet, gloves, and O2 cartridges."

The chest opens silently, the inside yellowed too. Picking up the orange helmet, he turns it in his hands. It reminds him of a motorcycle helmet, but the tinted visor goes all the way down, leaving no space other than where he'll shove his head in. Recessed holes run along its rim, and there are clamps on both sides. Circuitry goes over and under and down to the bottom. A center, teal stripe goes across the top to the rear.

He pulls it over his head. Latches automatically click into place around his neck, and the bottom seals around his collar, shrinking like the suit. He feels a quick stinging right above his spine. Something briefly hums, and warmth radiates over his body. The humming gradually quiets. The visor's clear from the inside, as if he's not wearing the helmet at all.

"Now put the gloves on," he hears Crews inside his helmet. As he does, Crews continues. "How's it feel to know I'm inside your head?"

"Not great." One glove, the other. Both seal.

"If it makes you feel any better, you can mute the short-wave anytime."

The O2 canisters are gray steel, a protruding bead at the top. Twisting around to find the slots, he slides in one after another until all four are secured. "Good to know."

A small timer appears on the bottom right of the visor. White numbers read 48:00:00.

"Guessing forty-eight hours is the amount of air I have?"

"You'd guess right. Feel lucky. If you weren't HUSK'd you'd only have sixteen."

Oh boy... "This should be a short trip then?"

"Uh huh. I wouldn't worry, forty-eight is more than enough. Plus, if you manage to get the ship going and the filters aren't busted, you won't have to worry about air anyway."

Jay glances into the box again. "What about that thing?"

"What thing?"

Jay pulls out the firearm. Even in the future they haven't found a better shape for a gun, though this one's more similar to a power drill than a Glock or pistol. The barrel is longer, no safety or cock; seemingly no ammo clip or a place to slide in rounds. Gray with blue hollows running up the handle, a red indentation down the barrel.

"Oh, yeah, that." Jay hears Crews slap his forehead. "Totally forgot."

On the other side of the grip are twelve glowing, yellow, slanted rectangles, and on the bottom of the grip is a silver divot. "Take it it only has twelve rounds?"

"Right."

"And to reload?"

"Wouldn't worry about that. Hell, wouldn't even be worried about the weapon either. Doubt you'll need it."

Jays holds it close to his waist and it jerks onto the black strip. He lets it go and it stays.

Damn, that's cool.

"Enough screwing around," Crews says. "Stand and look at the wall by the box. Little to the left. Perfect."

The room rattles. Something under Jay vibrates. Whooshing sounds overhead. Jay feels like if he could sweat he would be filling buckets. His hands clam up, but he's unsure if it's happening or if it's only in his mind.

"Now, once this opens, you'll follow the bridge to the *Candlewood's* airlock. It won't be online, so your O2 will kick in."

"Anything else?"

"Not that I'm aware of, but I'll tell you where to go once you get on board. Got it?"

"Uh huh." His eyes are wide and he's biting his bottom lip. Hasn't felt like this since first joining the police force.

"Wonderful."

A section of the wall slides skyward.

Holy...

"Shit."

A makeshift, triangular corridor connects the renter to the *Candlewood*. The walls are sheets of taut, glossy film, the floor honeycombed plastic, the beams corrugated scrap. It lowers a little when Jay steps onto it, as though walking upon pads floating on water. Along the top are long, cloudy lights not bright enough to cast shadows. Jay's unable to pull his gaze from the nothingness surrounding him.

His mouth open, eyes wide, he takes in the cosmos stretching for miles, miles, miles. Millions, billions of lights dot the celestial tapestry. In the impossibly far distance, he thinks he can see the Sun, the Moon, a bright red star—Mars—and a lighter blue one. On the opposite side, a titanic, sandy planet stretches higher than he can crane his head and lower than viewable from where Jay stands. It's like standing before... He can't fathom; larger than the biggest mountain, taller than any building imaginable, encompassing space in every direction. It seems hundreds of miles away yet close enough to touch.

He's having difficulty catching his breath, his heart pounding against his sternum and lodging in his throat.

"Keep moving, Jay."

He hasn't realized he stopped, hasn't realized he was pushing on the film with his hands, fingers forming divots in the material. He frantically views the cosmos for anything else, anything more; his curiosity untethered. Jay wants to push through the barrier, float into the ether, experience being among the inconceivable sights people only dreamed of in his time. A sliver of yearning forms in the recesses of his mind, like nostalgia, like a piece missing with him on the bridge. A loneliness screaming to be filled by someone he doesn't know.

"Jay," Crews cuts in. "Hurry the hell up, the connector can't stay out for too long. Remember, this is a renter; can't power everything at once."

He closes his mouth, blinks, and retreats to the center of the bridge. "Yeah," he whispers, shaking his head. "Sorry. Just... Just—"

"I get it, just get on the damn ship."

Jay picks up the pace to the end of the tunnel. The connector leads to an opening in the ship. The renter's harsh flood lights paint its corrugated hull, but within is darker than the space surrounding him.

"How do I turn on the lights?"

"You can't on the ship, not yet. But for your suit, at first, just think about it. Eventually, the suit will get familiar enough with your brain patterns to know when to do it without you even thinking about it. This tech covers everything—your boots, turning off/on short wave, etc. A benefit of not being human."

Lights... ON?

Lights outlining his visor blink to life, lancing through the murkiness, illuminating a bare, white floor.

Mags ON.

His boots suddenly feel heavier, but he can still move them, albeit slowly. Hesitantly stepping into the doorway, as though walking through ankle-deep mud, Jay crosses into the *Candlewood*.

I

48:00:00

C ASTING HIS LIGHT, HE glances around the empty, white room. It's similar to the one he left on the renter but larger. A metal bench runs along one wall, and against the other are stainless steel lockers. He pops one open. A suit like his own, the helmet drifting against the roof. It makes no noise when he shuts it. Going another two down, he finds the same thing. An indent runs around the edge of the room from the floor, up the walls to the ceiling. Frayed, transparent material sticks out of the track, swaying in the non-gravity.

Seems like someone ripped the barrier apart...

His hand remains on his weapon as he crosses onto gray floor-ing. No scratches or scuffs across it, no clothes or suits thrown carelessly, no indicators to show that anyone was rushing out of, or into, the ship.

Then why was the airlock ripped?

He rainchecks the question and enters a narrow hall with rigid, metal walls. Breathing heavy, Jay catches himself mouth-breathing and fixes it. The corridor opens up to—

"Damn."

"What?" Crews chirps in.

"This ship is way bigger inside than yours."

"No shit," he says. "Can't move cargo without something huge."

Vaulted ceilings meet in the center where a muted black rafter runs from the ship's front to its rear. It splinters like roots off into open doorways along the opposite side of the hall.

Jay walks into the middle, turning, taking it in, jaw slack. The walls are patched with long, square pieces of beaded, gray metal; the floor and bridge are the same, honeycombed and not cleanly cut, jagged. Dusk consumes the ship's stern, making it unviewable. His lights only illuminate the floor, gradually sloping down.

"You can ignore everything for now," Crews says. "Just get to the pilot bay. That's where everything's at."

Jay looks ahead. "Guessing that's in the bow?"

"Wow, look at you with your boating lingo."

"Is it there or not?"

"Yeah."

His steps make no sound, the boots not clanging against the metal underfoot. The only noise is his breathing, his heart pounding in his ears. Everything seems too clean, too sterile, as though the ship was simply turned off and abandoned, no foul play; yet something in Jay's false gut tells him there's more to the picture than what he can see.

Shallow ditches skirt the bridge where the walls curve down, meeting beams matching the center rafter.

Wonder what those are for...

They probably contain futuristic wiring, fibers, and microscopic technology unheard of, impossible, in his time. Things he can't imagine even now. It still feels unbelievable, surreal, when Jay ponders the present; where he's at, what he's doing, what and who he is. It opens his thoughts to even more questions about the universe as a whole—

Okay, okay. Don't get existential. Back to the job.

He shakes his head, clearing his mind. Ahead, open double-doors appear in the darkness. Beyond are two seats bolted to the ground, belts unstrapped and dangling loosely in the non-air, and a large, wide console of buttons, switches, and levers flanking a flat screen in the center, a keyboard in front of each seat. Along the walls are more tiny monitors, more knobs and things Jay hasn't a clue what their purpose is. Leaning over the console, Jay finds curving, concave windshields on the top and bottom.

"There's a lot here."

"In the pilot bay?"

"Uh huh..." He glances around the room, re-taking everything in.

"There should be a console—"

"Yup"

"—and a big screen in the middle with keyboards, yeah?"

"They're right in front of me." Jay's hesitant to touch anything for fear of blowing up the ship.

"Press a key on the right keyboard."

"Sure about that?"

"Positive."

He does, and the screen emits an electronic soft green. A white cursor appears at the top right.

"No color?"

"I'm not made of money, have to cut corners where I can." Crews sighs. "Anyway, it turning on means that at least the ship still has power. Now listen closely, Jay, and type in exactly what I say."

Peck by peck, Jay enters a string of commands Crews rattles off: one to override the power safety mode the *Candlewood* automatically activated when whatever happened, happened; another to initiate administrator access and permissions; a last one that will bring the ship back online if everything's working the way it ought to.

A force erupts from the door, throwing Jay against the console. His body's squeezed by a giant hand and his joints and muscles scream for mercy. Then it's over, gone as quickly as it came. Carefully, he straightens. Dim lights pop on overhead. An error reads on the monitor.

GRAVITY: ON / AIR FILTERS: ERROR — INACTIVE.

"Says the gravity's on, so should I undo the mags?"

"Yeah, go ahead. What about the air?"

Mags and lights OFF?

His boots become lighter. He lifts one foot then the other. The helmet lights extinguish. "Says there's an error, 'Inactive.'"

"Well shit. Guess you're sticking with the canisters."

"Should have enough air, right?"

"Yeah, yeah. Ship's not *that* big."

Glancing over his shoulder, Jay notices the tiny monitors are on. They're monochrome, static and white noise filling some while others remain empty. There are white-lettered titles on the lower left.

Mess Hall... Bunks... Mech Shop... Cargo... Engine Room... A row on the bottom shows white, speckled darkness, each named EXTR 1 through 10, respectively. The images are tiny, but Jay thinks he sees Crews's ship and the bridge receding back into the renter. *Must be the cameras outside the ship.*

Turning his attention back to the interior, three rooms are ransacked—Mess, Bunk, and Mech—whereas nothing can be seen in the Engine Room. The camera in Cargo has been covered in gunk, open splotches blurry. In the Mess, chairs and a round table are upturned, dinnerware and packets are strewn about, debris is heaped against the corner; where the crew sleeps, blankets and pillows spill out of cubbies inlaid into the wall. Some curtains torn and opened, others closed. From the low-definition feed, Jay believes he sees things piled in the beds and a closed door at the end of the hall. The Mech's Room is the same, swapping bed things for tools and blown open toolboxes vomiting gadgets over the floor. There's a ladder to the side descending into the Engine Room.

No bodies. Where's the crew?

He taps a few buttons in the hopes the other monitors turn on, but they don't.

"Where should I start? I can only see five rooms; the cameras in the others are broken or something."

"I said I'd tell you where to go first, Jay," Crews says. "You're the detective, so you figure out what the fuck happened on my ship. I'm not the one there—"

The intercom mutes, and Jay, grinning, leaves the Pilot's Bay.

Wonder what's behind the closed door?

Where he came in from—what he dubs the Main Hall—is still dark, as though the recessed lighting along the center rafter isn't strong enough to reach everywhere. The gutters parallel with the walkway; the crevices in the vaulted ceiling and the stern remain submerged in shadows. Jay enters the Mess Hall, and luckily, it's the first door from where he left.

Who woulda thought? It's a mess in here.

The monitor had made it look cleaner. The table on its side blocks what seems like a restroom; a handful of waist-high, silver stools with rings on their legs poke out from piles of hydration packs and freeze-dried food. Odds and ends—beige dinnerware, plates and bowls and other things—are crumbled by a broken, small, open freezer. Food's smeared and caked to the ceiling, alongside long scratches and dents in the metal.

At least the lights in the middle weren't destroyed.

Jay kicks away trash, revealing a black stain with a rainbow sheen—an oil spill, slick and wet looking. Crouching, he runs his fingers over it, but it doesn't come away. Completely dry. He gives it another try but still nothing, like it's a part of the floor.

Instinctively, he raises his fingers to his nose, but remembers the helmet, the suit; then remembers he *can't* smell. He wipes his hand on his leg while he stands, and turns to an off-shooting open corridor.

"Know anything about black mold?" he asks Crews.

The short wave activates, and Crews comes through mid-sentence: "Mold?"

The corridor is the Bunks. Six on both sides, three each wall. "Yeah, I think I found some in the cafeteria... Can space food get moldy?"

"Shouldn't," he says. "It's not bio-organic, not what you'd call a 'whole food.' Tons of artificial preservatives, flavoring, etc. GMO'd to the teeth to stay edible for years."

A torn curtain is pulled aside in a bottom cubby, revealing a disheveled, pine green blankets and two pillows. No stains or blood or tears in the mattress; no objects or items to tell who slept there last.

Looks like someone woke up in a hurry though.

"How many were on the crew?"

"Five, I think. Maybe six. What they put down in the log isn't always accurate. Sometimes they pick up strays who need some money or a way out and don't track them."

The next one looks untouched. He draws back the blue curtain. There are pillows stacked in the corner, the blanket folded underneath.

Wonder how it stayed like that?

"Isn't that risky?" he says. "You never know how people are, especially cooped up like this."

The last two are torn asunder. Blankets and mattresses and

pillows are ripped apart, all stuck together by the same gunk Jay found in the previous room. Everything's helter-skelter, unable to be unglued and pieced out or inspected. This stuff is dry too.

"I guess," he says. "But people need to make a living, too, and as long as the job's done, who gives a shit?"

"Is that why you don't ask questions about shipments either?"

The substance is spilled from the beds, streaming toward and stopping at the closed door. Jay isn't sure if he saw it before on the monitor and it didn't register, or maybe he's rustier in observance than he initially believed. The light gives it a sheen, and again he futilely tries to wipe some away with his boot.

"Hey, hey—don't get the wrong idea here. We ask questions, have them fill out forms and sign waivers. If they happen to lie, that's on them. We're not liable."

Jay draws his weapon before nearing the door. When he gets to the door, it slides open automatically, revealing a closet. Sighing, he sets the gun back to his waist. Blue-gray chests in rows of three, nine in total, line the walls. "And you check every container, right? To make sure they *didn't* lie?"

Jay isn't sure why he's still talking to Crews...

Probably to fill the silence. It's damn eerie here.

When he goes to open one in the middle, the part facing him slides down and back. Inside are a few sheets of paper with the name *Brendon Falls*. Looks like lab papers of some sort. Jay pushes them aside, reaching further in, swiping away pens and a pair of glasses. There's not much else but a couple faded logo shirts balled in the back.

Moving on to the one above, the middle chest closes by itself.

"Well, no. No one does, not only us. Only the big players in the game do that because they can afford it. Plus, they have AI doing the nitty-gritty work, not actual people."

"Isn't it cheaper doing it that way? It seemed to be when I

was alive. All the big companies used technology to replace workers."

He finds a pair of gray sweatpants, a pine green tank-top, a wireless bra, hair ties with wiry blonde hair stuck to a few, and navy blue slippers with *Rose* written in the insole. Nothing else with identification.

Jay turns to the other column, opens the center.

Inside's a heavily used tablet that won't turn on, *Kat Wilkinson* labeled on its scratched, gunmetal back. In the rear is a rolled-up sweatshirt, fuzzy socks, and... a small round device with a matte, inlaid screen. The back is labeled *Prop. of Med Bay*. Pressing a button on its side, a short prong slides out of the bottom. Pressing it again retracts it. *What is this?* Another button on the opposite side dimly illuminates the screen. Jay's able to scroll with it, skimming a list of scientific terminology, numbers, and percentages—*Glucose: 78 mg/dL, BUN: 10mg/dL, Creatinine: 0.9 mm/dL*—but he stops at the bottom, highlighting: *hCG: 70 mIU/mL (Pregnant: Y).*

Shit. His breath catches in his throat.

Crews has been talking, but he hasn't been listening. He hears the butt-end, "...but you shit in one hand and wish in another, right?"

"Did you know one of your crew was pregnant?" he says, the frog in his throat dwindling enough for him to inhale deeply.

"Uh..." he stammers, then says, "*No.* We strictly prohibit pregnant folks from working in transportation."

"What about when on board? People here for so long, not much to do, hormones run high..."

"It happens, but when they sign on for the contract, they agree that they have been taking one of the many pills or shots or devices to stop it from happening, or they've had the goods removed to ensure it *can't* happen."

"Wow."

"Yeah, yeah. Sounds bad, but space is no place for giving birth or kids. Especially in a transporter like that. There's a med bay, but it's not fucking equipped for that sort of thing, you know?"

Jay nods, sliding the device back into the chest. He scans over the room again before leaving.

––––––––––––

Jay looks left and right at the doorway in the Main Hall. Now that he's found the black stuff, he gives everything another look over, finding no trace out here.

It might be hidden by the shadows.

But when he activates his lights, they still can't reach the precipice of the vaulted ceiling. Flicking them off, a question pops into his head.

"So, you ship things, right?"

"Retrieve, transport, and deliver, yeah."

"Do you remember the last shipment you received?"

"If it was logged, yeah, but it wasn't. The ship went MIA two weeks before you were brought on. And with the power down except for, I guess, the emergency backup, the data relay was down too."

"Couldn't you check now? Wouldn't the info be queued to be sent once the power's back on?"

"It *should,* but if it has, I have no way of checking it. It relays to the office back on DS5, and I didn't bring an APC with me."

Jay walks into the hall, facing the ship's rear. "Aren't there still smartphones? Everyone had one at all times back when I was alive."

"That's basically what an APC is. Arm Personal Computer. I mean, there's internal relays and communications, automatic ways to talk to someone over audio through the use of an implanted chip, but those only reach so far. An APC can piggyback on the long-wave system that runs from planet to planet, send audio, text, files, etc., but they're pricey. Most regular people can't afford them, especially in DS5."

He moves down the walkway and stops before an empty doorway. "You said you transport and deliver anything without questions, right?"

"Uh huh."

"So, what about human trafficking?"

"People are commodities, depending on their skillset. It's not technically illegal as long as they're not children or used for slavery."

"And if it's against their will without you knowing? Would you still ask no questions?"

"Do you really want to know?"

A shiver of revulsion goes through Jay as he crosses the threshold.

II

44:35:51

A HALL LEADS TO what must be the Mech Shop. A stainless-steel tool bench runs across one wall. By the opposite wall is a square opening in the floor and a ladder poking out. The floor's no longer honeycombed but metal, a railing at the end of it. It's a disaster of strewn about tools and food; hooks along the baseboard over the tool bench are empty. Jay steps over and around wrenches and screwdrivers and what look like futuristic power tools. There are devices that he has never seen before; one reminds him of a flashlight combined with an apple peeler, another looks as if a can opener and a power drill had an ugly child.

Looking over the railing, there's only vast nothingness. His headlights come on, but they don't reach far enough, maybe a glimpse of a quick gleam.

Think I saw something down there.

He turns back, lights switching off, and kicks around the debris finding no smears underneath.

"What was the mechanic like?" he says to Crews.

"Uh... Only met him once. Big tan guy with long, gray hair. Built like an ox. Kinda looked like one too. I think he's a Martian or from the Belt, but I don't know. Quiet type, kept to himself.

I barely meet the crews, just the captains, and that's only for a few minutes to make sure their logs are above board."

Jay glances at the tool bench again then the floor. Bites his lower lip. Not knowing what to look for, he can't be certain if anything is missing or taken. *Not much you can do.* He goes to the ladder and carefully starts climbing down.

He descends into a narrow space cut from the ship's hull, but midway Jay stops when he comes across a small cubby. A blanket's balled up in the corner, a pillow pushed against it. A small screen in the wall in another corner and a flickering tablet below.

What is this...

A nude, muscular man takes up the monochrome screen, and shadowed tendrils come out of the bottom of the artwork. He thinks the title across the top reads: *Forbidden Tales From Below*.

Different strokes for different folks. Everyone needs a little alone time. Jay shrugs, flicks it back to where he found it, and continues.

The ladder ends a foot above a catwalk. Darkness consumes everything. Lights on, he peers down, the railing flanking the floor shining. He drops, lands, still unsettled without the clanging of metal.

It's like he's standing in a deep cavern. His lights barely pierce the thick gloam pressing upon him, blanketing his joints and muscles. His heart rate increases, and if he could, he'd be sweating. The catwalk leads to another descending ladder.

Jay scans the emptiness. Before going down, he takes a deep breath.

The journey's not as long as the last, and soon he's on solid ground. If he was in a cavern before, now it truly feels like he's underearth—beneath *something* titanic. Every direction is an abyss.

"What's below the Mech Shop?" he says, a little too late.

"Engine Bay and EPE."

"Is the room massive?"

"Biggest place on the ship, yeah. Old school, so the engine is enormous, unlike newer models. And there's nowhere else to have the EPE. It's a legal requirement, so it was crammed in wherever it would fit."

Jay thinks he hears a noise and spins around. Takes him a moment to remember there's no sound here.

Calm down, Jay; your mind's fucking with you.

"EPE?"

"Emergency Pod Evacuation, for when shit really hits the fan."

Unsure which direction to follow, Jay anchors himself to the ladder and goes straight. If he's right, he's nearing the ship's front. "Were any used before it went dark?"

"None were activated. They run on emergency relays, so even if the ship's power's down, info's dumped to the station."

Glances right. Nothing.

Glances left. Nothing.

Teeth clenched.

Slow step by slow step...

Something reflects his lights, and Jay freezes, eyes wide, hand on weapon. He focuses on what's before him, and his fear drains. He expected futuristic monstrosities, things that were in movies and books, but it's only a body. A corpse. He'd seen plenty of those when he was a detective, but not quite like this.

Plastered by a heap of solidified ichor, ivory bones protrude and poke out like curved, broken stalagmites. Tattered pieces of indiscernible clothing, or possibly a spacesuit, cling to pointed edges from bone charred by what may be fire. Some shreds on the ground, but there's nothing among the scraps to ID the body.

"Found someone," he says.

"Who? Where?"

"I don't know who, but in a corner of the Engine Room."

"What's it look like?"

Jay stands over the mangled corpse. "Covered in hard, black gunk. Looks like whoever it was exploded from the inside out. Can't see any limbs or a head."

"Shit—wonder how the hell that happened... Did you search it?"

"Uh..." He tilts his head. The corpse refracts like a gas spill beneath light. "Honestly, I don't know how I would."

"Well, figure it the fuck out. There's probably something important there."

He doesn't respond as he crouches. Jay reaches for the body but halts before a prickled patch of ivory. He doesn't want to touch it, doesn't want to take the chance of tearing open his suit, doesn't want to feel it against his skin...

But money's money, and given a second life when the first one didn't seem all that great isn't something I want to fuck up.

His fingers scratch away the sludge. Feels like stone but comes away like ash, powdery, caking to his gloves. Dust drifts and motes dance in the light. Sighing with relief, he digs his hand into the person. Soot halfway up his forearm, he finds nothing but more ash... Wait, underneath a hardened clump there's something solid. Pinching it, he pulls his hand out and stands.

Wiping away what he can, he discovers what looks like a memory stick. He vaguely recalls them from days before storage and media became wireless, all in the cloud.

"I found something that looks like a memory card."

"Probably their MLID. Are there red copper bits on the bottom?"

"Yeah."

"Then that's what it is. It's a chip built into all the suits the crews wear so they can keep track of each other while onboard. If things go sideways, everyone can know who was where and view the logs of what happened."

"Does it have video?"

"Nah, only audio, and even then sometimes that doesn't work. They have to manually turn it on. The captain had a V-MLID, though; too expensive for everyone else."

"Do I have one in my suit?"

Crews laughs. "*Fuck* no, you're not that special."

Jay leaves the body and heads back to the ladder.

"Would the computer in the Pilot's Room read it?"

"It should, yeah, but the mech had an APC—everyone did, a cost I unfortunately couldn't ignore—so there might be one in their place somewhere."

Jay gets back to the ladder and climbs.

He brushes aside debris and sets the chip on the tool bench, then sifts through the things on the floor.

"What's an APC look like?"

"You'll know it when you see it."

Great.

On his knees, he moves things around, revealing nothing that looks like any sort of a computer. No smears either. Lying flat, he peers under the tool bench's bottom shelf. He moves more instruments and clutter out of the way, and against the back wall is something that looks like it *could* be a computer. Stretching his arm the furthest it'll go, he snatches and pulls it out.

It has curved ends with rounded edges around an opening, black with gray accents, dry ichor splashed over the top. It reminds Jay of what gauntlet knights once wore in the medieval

40

era. The piece within the curve is transparent, revealing reddish-brown circuitry embedded within green.

"Think I found it."

"Great, put it on."

Arm... Oh!

Jay wipes away the soot and slides it onto his forearm. The wrist cover adjusts to his forearm automatically, and the outside cover pops like a trunk. He pushes it up, revealing a computer screen encompassing the entirety of the board. Small ports and slots are on the side of the monitor, and he grabs the MLID, finds one that fits it, and slides it in.

Click.

———

The screen comes to life, showing a three-dimensional, green grid of the *Candlewood*. Each room given corresponding names. A red dot appears in the Mess. No voices or sounds except for faint chitter-chatter, gradually ebbing into silence, and heavy breathing. The dot moves into the Main Hall, then to the Mech Room, where Jay now stands.

"These people are intolerable." Jay assumes it's the mechanic speaking, voice gravely and guttural, as though shrapnel could talk. "Can't wait 'till this job's done and I can get back to the Belt. Fuckin' miss sleeping; fuckin' miss fuckin'..."

The dot stops moving.

"Wonder if I should even sign up for the next trip," he huffs. "After the cap opened that damn container, shit's just becoming too fuckin' wild."

There's a clanging or banging noise like feet kicking against ladder rungs.

"Who the hell's down there?" the man spits, then muses. "Do one of those Hoppers think they're sneaky?"

"Hey, asshole! What do you think you're doing—"

The audio goes ballistic. Jay winces and quickly pulls his arm away even though the sound is inside his helmet. A high-pitched, electrical whine, shrieking, rising and rising, crescendoing when a deep-throated scream explodes and over-whelms everything... Then it crackles out, becoming white noise.

The on-screen dot gets to the catwalk, crosses it, then goes down into the Engine Room. At the bottom, it goes to the front of the ship, and stops.

The audio ceases and the screen winks out.

———————

A chill trickles down Jay's spine as he shuts the screen. It be-comes level with the wrist band.

"What the hell was that?" he whispers.

"No damn idea," Crews says. "But take the APC and MLID with you, try to find the others."

He listens and leaves.

III

40:51:27

H E MAKES FOR ONE doorway down, a room that wasn't shown on the security cams. Jay stops before the threshold, exhaling air he didn't know he's holding.

There's so much I just don't know... So many things that seem way above my pay grade. I was a detective, sure, but that was hundreds of years ago... This is—whatever it is—something else entirely... Exploded, petrified corpses? Spaceships? And what about that black shit, that man's screams? What the hell happened? He rests his hand on the weapon's grip.

No sounds, no air, no damn answers for anything...

Get through it, Jay. Hurry it up. If you don't figure out what went on on this ship, then fine, whatever. Who's to say you didn't try? It's not like Crews's going to double-check your investigation. Be sloppy if you want. Make getting out of this place priority number one.

Jay enters the room.

———

He is wrong to believe the Mess and Bunks are chaos. What must be the Medical Bay is a hell-scape in human proportions.

Wraps, gauze, and other medical supplies spill from torn open emergency kits hanging on the walls, thrown across the floor. Black splotches hang from the ceiling, covering some of the weak lights, stalactites reaching almost to his head. More ink slapped and streaked across the walls, collecting in the far corner as though that's where it originates from. Paper curtains and plastic sheets are in shreds, and scalpels, tongs, compressor cuffs, and other tools are tangled in a hodge-podge of litter. The few machines are smashed into pieces of burnt plastic and glass; beds and chairs and—*fucking* everything's destroyed.

Beneath a white sheet soaked-through by dark fluid, Jay finds another clumpy gore of broken, protruding bones and hardened sludge. Exploded like the other, flayed, charred spikes issuing from the core of the crew member, bits of white poking out. No head or skull to be seen, hardly anything to signify it was a person at all.

I'm so glad I have a helmet on.

This thought gives way to others: remembering the diseases from when he was alive, some airborne, some by touch; the hell they wrought upon the Earth while the powers that be scrambled to protect their cash flow, while lowly servants did nothing and let the diseases blow through their population like a tornado.

Also kind of relieved I'm only a copy, that if I were to get sick and die I could still come back. Be alive. In another HUSK, maybe, but still...

His head starts to ache from unraveling the complexities of past, current, and potential future life. Death as he knows it is seemingly non-existent, only a pause between the past and future. Crews is talking, and he catches the end: "... and the food, God was it good."

"Uh huh." He hunkers and plunges his hand into the hardened

goo in the corner. The bottom interior is still soft, malleable, and he feels something sticking up that may be a MLID. He pinches it and pulls. There's some resistance before it snaps like elastic, and a plume of ash blows out around his arm.

It envelopes his visor, and at first it's nothing, his helmet and suit air-tight and sealed, impossible to get through. Then something floral hits his nose; lilac, lilac fills his nostrils.

His wife's name, *Nicole,* unfurls quietly from the well of his subconscious, and he's cast into a kaleidoscopic vat of overlapping, vibrant, cloying colors, and as the void below reaches him it shatters like glass and he's

in a hotel room. The French doors leading to the balcony are open, white curtains billowing, morning sunlight spilling through and filling their room with radiance. The floral aroma is everywhere, but there's no flowers to be found. His hands are in his lap, and he looks at his palms. A gold band on his ring finger, left hand, and in the other is his cell phone, "1 Missed Call" on the screen.

"Jay, you ready?" a smooth voice says from behind.

He closes his hands and turns on the chair, catching a glance of the unmade bed, pillows toppled to the floor, blankets and sheets tangled. Nicole stands in the bathroom doorway, wearing a black fitted dress that accentuates her curves, closing the back of an earring.

Her blue eyes meet his, and she smirks. "Are you wearing that out?"

"Uh..." He realizes he's in a white t-shirt and plaid boxers, hairy legs and long feet. "I guess not."

"Well, hurry up," she says, coming to him and putting her hands around the back of his head, fingers playing with his hair. He relishes the floral scent now that it's near.

Nicole notices the cell phone. "Who called?"

"Work."

"Don't they know you're not even in the same city?"

"Yeah, but that doesn't matter to them."

"Sometimes I wish you wouldn't have taken that promotion."

"Same..."

"Enough about that. Get up and get dressed." She looks down at him. Their eyes lock. "We're going to be late to lunch as it is, since someone kept me in bed longer than I should've been."

"Yeah, well, you see... We're on vacation, kind of." He laughs. She does too.

"I'm not complaining, but c'mon, we're seeing your sister after, remember? The whole reason we flew down here."

"Oh, right... Ashleigh." He looks at the floor and puts his hand on hers, rubbing pale, lotioned skin with his thumb. Weight blankets him, the verge of tears rushing through him. "Hope she's not pissed when we show up."

"I just hope she's doing okay."

"Me too."

Jay reels back, holding the MLID, throat tight. "That *smell*," he gasps. It takes him a beat for his mind to adjust to reality, his focus to what he was doing. Feels like hours have passed, but going by the O2 counter, it's only been a minute, two tops.

"What do you mean, smell?"

Jay shakes his head and wipes the gunk from his hand on the wall. "What do you mean?"

It won't get off him, but he finds a towel on the floor beneath a turned over stool. Uses it to wipe most of it away, though some still stains his glove.

"You *can't* smell," Crews says. "You're a HUSK without odor receptors installed, remember? And you're in a suit that's not open to the outside. It's impossible."

He unfolds the APC screen, pops out the mechanic's MLID,

and switches it with the newly discovered one.

"Well, I just did, so..."

"Did you smell anything before right now? Are you losing more oxygen than usual?"

Jay thinks about the dinner they had. The soup Crews ate. The people in the street he passed. He doesn't remember any scents but also doesn't remember if he tried to smell anything anyway. But the image of his wife standing before him, their hands touching, burns in his mind. Ignoring it, checking the air timer—which seems to be dwindling at a normal rate—he says: "Don't think so to both."

"Can you smell anything now?"

He sniffs, hoping for flowers, but he smells nothing. "No."

"Huh... Okay, whatever. Probably just your mind fucking with you, but let me know if anything else like that happens again."

"Will do," he says. "Anyway, I found another MLID in the Med Bay."

"Wonderful."

———

A pink dot appears where he stands. No audio for a while, then: "...Nurses always get the short end," a monotone voice says lowly. A man, it sounds like. Something taps against something else, electronic beeping in the background. An EKG, maybe? Scribbling, scratching, like pen on paper. "Can't believe he didn't listen..."

A groan.

"Doin' okay, Harty?"

Jay hears the sound of metal clanging on metal, grinding against something. The swish of a curtain pulled aside, rings gliding on a pole.

Another voice. Quiet, polite. "May I have some more pain

meds?" Another groan. "I don't understand why I'm like this."

"It happens sometimes," the monotone voice says. "With false G, the body does a lot of weird things."

Rustling again, cloth on cloth.

"Sorry," the nurse says. "Not much room to maneuver—if only health was prioritized more—here you go."

A curtain is thrown back, the nurse saying, "What're doing here, C—"

The audio goes ballistic, like before. Shrill whining forces Jay to wince and pull his arm away instinctively. It tears into static shrieking, like tin being sawed apart. Bits of screaming cut in and out, more than one person. A barrage of frenzied noise, like a mic plummeting down a well, until silence abruptly comes.

The screen goes blank.

"You get all that?" he asks, glancing over the room again.

"Yeah. Seems like whatever got the mech got the nurse and someone else too."

"Sounds like it..." Jay maneuvers through the debris. "But the timeline, I'm not sure about."

"Does that matter?"

He crouches, gingerly tugs at a curtain's hem. Doesn't move. "Kind of." Tries again and gets the same results. He gives up and stands. "It would give me an idea of where whoever or whatever came from. If this place got hit first, then the thing likely came from the rear. But if the mech was first—"

"It'd come from the bow, right?"

"More than likely."

But there aren't any breaks in the windshields and no other way to get into the pilot's room except through the door. Aren't any smudges there either. Whatever it is, and for whatever reason, it probably came from the stern and worked its way down.

"He said 'C'—is there anyone on the ship whose name starts

with C?"

"Uh..." Crews stammers. "Not that I can remember."

Jesus, he doesn't even know his own staffs' first names.

"But maybe he was saying 'Captain.'"

"Who was Harty then?"

"Don't know. Maybe a Hopper; maybe someone hired for a short contract."

C... C... Captain could be it.

Jay stops before the mangled body of what remains of the nurse. He recalls the floral scent, the flash of memory of being in a hotel room with his wife. His finger twitches, and a longing blooms in the back of his head. He wants to reach his hand in again, wants to inhale the unknown fumes, wants to discover if more memories, more *senses*, will return if he rummages in the decay. It's a couple transfixed minutes, until his reverie's broken by Crews.

"So where you going next?"

"The Captain's Quarters."

IV

37:38:59

T HERE'S ONE OTHER ROOM besides the captain's before the floor slopes down where shipments are taken in. Jay checks it before moving in. It's a storage closet that appears like a tornado ran through it with food packages, hydration packs, some medical supplies like bandages and gauze strewn about.

"Make it to the cap's place yet?" Crews says.

"No, checking out this space food."

Jay takes one down, reads the side label.

Peanut Butter and Banana (Synthetically and Artificially Flavored).

Contains: Lab-Grown Nuts, Wheat, Soy, Dairy, Eggs, Fish.
DIST. & SOLD EXCLUSIVELY BY:
EDULIS, CO.
ELUSK-12, MOON M-0012

The enormous list of ingredients is too tiny to read, and Jay can't imagine eating a freeze-dried lump of chalky space food that would taste anywhere as delicious to the original. And why would eggs, soy, and fish be in a PB&B?

"Why?"

He sets it back, grabs another.

Key Lime Pie (Synthetically and Artificially Flavored). It contains all the ingredients the previous one did, and another he's never heard of before: *Phlagn*. Sounds disgusting, bringing images of deep sea, of silt and nocturnal fish. He grimaces and returns it.

"Curious," he says.

"About that space garbage? C'mon, you ain't got time to burn."

The door slides closed when he steps away. He turns back and continues on.

"More than enough to read a few labels."

"If you say so."

"Hey," he says. "I have a question though. Are memories wiped when HUSK'd?"

"Yup. Not all, like motor functions, what things are, etc. But specific, personal memories, yeah."

"So not what my favorite food was, or who my first kiss was, or what my job was like day to day?"

"Those are all wiped clean during the export," Crews says. "Not in all cases, since everyone's needs are different, but for jobs like this it helps having no memories to create biases or other shit like that. Like if I needed someone to work construction on a tall-ass building, I wouldn't want the HUSK to have a memory of fear of heights."

"Got it, so it creates good workers, basically?"

"Basically."

Jay isn't sure if he feels comfortable with this new information. In some cases, he's sure past loved ones are HUSK'd so they can be together again, or celebrities and artists brought back for media purposes... But for the majority, they're creating ants, drones, single-minded individuals who look like humans but aren't, hired by slumlords and companies to do a job that they would otherwise not do if they had to do it themselves... He shakes his head. It's not much different from what he can remember from when he was alive, just more straightforward.

Doesn't matter now, does it? At least I still have my personality, if this is who I was before, because honestly, I can't remember... But what about that room, my wife, my sister? The lilac? Better not say anymore about it going forward.

Hardly paying attention, he crosses the walkway but halts when sludge overcomes the floor. He recoils.

"Shit!"

"What?" Crews shouts. "What happened?"

Looking up, he finds the entire doorway sealed by fresh ichor slowly pouring in rivulets into the hall. "Think I found where the stuff originated."

Helmet lights kick on, and the syrup reflects splotches of the white light. Jay puts his hand on his weapon. This near, the purplish emptiness gives him vertigo, like he's standing before the edge of an abyss. It continues to push out, sinking beneath the grated floor, hardening in real-time into bulging shapes before his feet. It cools like lava, like lard forced through a pipe...

I don't want to go in there.

"Did you go in yet?"

Hell no.

"Jay?"

"No," finally says. "I haven't."

"What's the hold up?"

"There's so much of it... I don't... I can't."

"Look, this's a job; you're being *paid* to do this. Plus, I don't even know why you're afraid, you can't fucking actually die."

Jay draws the weapon, raises it in one trembling hand while the other hesitantly reaches for the door. The rail it would slide on is jammed, but a wide enough opening allows his fingers through. Tugging, cracks spider-webbing through the dry sections, the door gives, and he pulls and shoves it fully open.

He sighs with relief when nothing explodes over him.
Unheeded, the goop bubbles, unfurling out more.
Stepping over it, he enters the quarters.

The stuff, dry, coats the walls, the floor, the ceiling, and forms
a wall midway into the room. If he was claustrophobic he'd be
losing his damn mind. Jay places his weapon back to his waist.
His lights cast opaque circles over the black, and tiny ash motes
swirl from below. No furniture or tools to be found, to be used
to break down the wall, so he picks away a little with his finger.

Wind whistles through the newly created hole. There
shouldn't be any noise since there's no air… Jay peeks. Uncurling
flakes of ash rise from a void, a nothingness somehow *darker*
than where Jay is. Without noticing, his face is pulled nearer
to the hole, his visor hitting the barrier. Looking up, he only
catches a glimpse of a scattershot of puncture holes in the
ceiling.

He pulls away and opens the APC to check out the map.

*Is there another room above here? A type of crawl space or air
duct?*

The map shows there's nothing above where he is, just outer
space.

But shouldn't everything be pulled in then? Like a vacuum?

"Yeah," Crews says, and Jay doesn't realize he said it aloud.
"You should be dead, my guy. Same with the ship's internals.
Everything yanked out like guts from a turkey."

Jay turns back to the hole, but it's already sealed by a fresh
glaze of tar. Not wanting to test his luck, he backs out of the
room, careful not to slip.

Jay looks over the map again. Pilot Bay, Mess and Bunks, Med and Mech, Engine, Cap's Place, and Storage Locker #1. He's checked them all, still as lost as he was when he started. There are three other rooms: Storage Locker #2, Rec Room, and the Cargo Bay. Jay figures it's not worth checking the storage locker since it'll likely be the same as Locker #1. He imagines the Rec Room will be similar to the others. He needs to cut to the chase and not waste any more time, even with over thirty hours left of air. *Getting off this ship is priority one.*

It's clear something happened. Something attacked the staff—who or what, he has no damn idea—and killed them. But it seems to have begun from the last shipment they picked up. The mechanic said something about the captain screwing with it, and the nurse likely was saying 'Captain' before she imploded. Not to mention the last room he inspected was nothing more than an incubator for the sludge, some type of breeding ground.

So the place I'll probably find some answers is...

V

"**S**O YOU STILL DON'T know what the last shipment is?"

"Not a damn clue," Crews says. "No way to get into the station's database from here. But, even if I could, it might not be logged."

"Why wouldn't it be?"

The floor moves downwards, the vaulted ceiling steadily growing in height. The overhead lights barely touch the ground, but Jay's light helps cut through the gloom.

"Because a crew can do whatever they want, to be honest. No one's looking over their shoulder or double-checking if everything's done by the book. If they pick up something illegal or unfavorable and decide not to include it in the logs, then how the fuck would I know it was done? I got other shit to do. I'm not a damn babysitter."

The floor flattens and comes to a dead end. A wall towers over him, a computer array at the bottom. To his right's a giant sliding door, dented and scratched. It reminds Jay of a garage door but on a much bigger scale. There's a normal-sized door inlaid within it. He checks the computer first by poking on the sticky keyboard, but the screen remains dead.

He opens the smaller door and enters.

Floodlights lining the upper wall paint the room in sterile light, the ceiling dark. Enormous metal containers stand like monoliths throughout the room, casting wide, flat shadows across the scuffed steel floor. Names and dates and other information are branded into their side, and on the adjacent side are circular protrusions ringed by red lights. Tucked into the corner by the door are vests strung on silver wiring running to what look like big, flat clamps. Nearby is a machine that seems like a forklift, though it has lifts on the top and sides, not only the bottom.

"*Sender: Mills Rock, LLC. To: Jezos Planetary Construction Weight: 25XT,*" Jay reads aloud from one container, meandering between the narrow passage between them.

"*Sender: FSE, INC. To: N.L Technologies. Weight: 13.5XT* —What's XT mean?"

"Multiplied Tons. We got tired of putting all the zeros and decimals. Not much else changed; higher number is heavier, lower is lighter."

It doesn't seem there's any rhyme or reason to where the containers are placed. Haphazardly set wherever they could shove them, Jay believes. Glancing between cargo and the floor, which is still clear of sludge, he moves around a shipment to the rear of the bay.

A giant door, like the one before, encompasses the back wall. *Must lead outside.*

A box up to his waist sits nearby. **WASTE** is in bold letters on its facing side, and it has a circular protrusion on top, not on the side like the others.

"Why does this say waste on it?"

"Those are potentially hazardous things that can't properly be stored or repurposed."

"Ah, so like..."

"Shit, sewage, etc., typically. Dumbass kids sometimes send them as pranks."

"Wonderful," Jay says, turning—

Filth slaps the floor before his feet. He looks up...

"Shit."

"Didn't I already say that's what it was?"

"No, not that."

"So you really don't know what they picked up, or possibly who?"

"No idea."

He can't imagine that many people were on the ship. The *Candlewood*'s large, but it doesn't seem too strenuous or complex for a skeleton crew. And knowing Crews, he wouldn't spend more money for more bodies. So, what the hell's plastered to the ceiling in a coagulation of charred, jutting bones and coagulated treacle must be either undocumented crew members or people who were just there for a ride. Pitch encompasses almost the entire ceiling, ending near the floodlights. Ribcages are cresting waves; imploded skulls are intertwined with vertebrae and ligaments within spiraling tendrils; sternums and femurs and pelvises appear exploded and torn into pieces, giving way to viny black unfurling from their centers.

And now that he's seen it, Jay glances around to find more of it on the floor and around the containers, splattering their tops. Shadows kept them hidden; he was too distracted by the shipping labels and Crews to look hard enough.

He feels a presence, eyes on him from somewhere, and draws his weapon. The floor rattles weakly. Stops. Rattles.

"Hello?" he calls out.

"You talking to me?" Crews says.

He doesn't respond and turns off the mic.

Creeping, he follows the vibrations. The stronger they feel tells him he's on the right track; the weaker he ignores. He sidesteps through the tight spaces around a cluster of four containers at least twelve feet high. A dry layer of ichor weaves from floor to wall to ceiling. A row of containers blocks his path, but he shimmies along the wall, soot rubbing onto his suit. Metal scratches his weapon.

The vibrations become stronger.

If he could sweat, Jay would be drenched. If his mouth could be dry, his tongue would feel like sandpaper. He briefly misses those sensations, the physical aspects of fear, of hesitation, of the unknown... Then it's gone. *Why would I want those things?*

Jay comes out into an area between the far corner, opposite the door. Shadows are thick there, the floodlights do not reach. Headlights lance through—Jay ducks almost too late when a metal rod whizzes past his head. It hits the wall, rolls, and stops against a container.

Looks again to find a woman tucked into the divot. She has a mangled arm dripping dark blood raised before her laboring chest, her hand shielding her eyes. No helmet, no suit, yet she's breathing... She's alive, barely. He keeps his budding questions in check.

"Turn off that fucking light," she spits. Oil bubbles from the corners of her mouth.

He does.

"Who was that?" Crews says in his ears. "Who's alive? Jay? Jay!"

He must've not muted the intercom correctly before, but he does now.

"Thanks," she says.

"No problem, but who are you?"

"Kat. Who're you?"

"Jay."

"You a real person...? I've hallucinated a ton since this clus-terfuck," she waves her hand in front of herself as though pre-senting something, "popped off."

"I'm a HUSK," he says, nearing, putting the gun to his waist. Closer, he makes out her distended belly, her other arm with-ered and shredded to tatters.

"Close enough," she huffs. "What're you doing here?"

He laughs. "Came to find out what happened. What about you?"

"Oh, you know." She grins, revealing oily teeth. "Just relaxing."

"So, what happened to you, Kat?"

She coughs out colorless phlegm, dribbling down her chin. "Picked up something we shouldn't have."

Not wanting to push too much, ease into the core of the situation, he changes the subject. "What was your job on the ship?"

"Just about everything: moving, shipping, carrying, cleaning, and data-logging. Only thing I couldn't—" She hacks. "—pilot, but even the pilots didn't even pilot. The ship flies its damn self most of the time."

"Where was your last pick-up?"

"No clue, can't remember. Somewhere on the outskirts of the Sola, I think. Heading for a pit stop on Phobos before a drop-off on the Moon."

It's surreal to hear her speak about planets like they're places in a city, like they're common and not a huge deal. Momentarily, Jay's in awe of space travel, of how it all works now, but he returns to reality quickly and repeats the question. "So what happened to you?"

"Like I said, we picked up something we shouldn't have. Weren't paying attention during the shipment, lost among the others. Checked out in the inspection though. But, Capt just *had* to look at what was inside."

"What was it?"

"Don't know," she says. "No one did, or does... Everything went to shit after that, though." She nods to the ceiling, to herself.

Kat winces as a hole tears between her splayed legs, and gelatinous, viscous goo spills out. A gnarled, dehydrated form settles in the dark afterbirth. All wrinkles and indents, rooty, skin almost matching the gore it lies in. Her belly dwindles, dwindles... She places her hand to it, rubbing weakly.

She's going.

Jay wants to let her be, to let her pass quietly, but he has one more question pressing against his lips. Something's been in the back of his mind since he left Z'teehs. He forces out, "What do you know about the owner of the ship? Crews?"

She opens her mouth but vomits tar. "Fine." Words lost to spillage. "Eco—" More, drenching the front of her already-soaked clothes. Her chest pumps faster, shuttering. "Would get out—" Her eyes widen, sclera blackening, and her mouth gapes as the rest of her words are lost to gurgling.

Jay reaches for her but stops. He shouldn't touch. He can't save her. He could be infected by whatever she has, and what could he do for her if he could? He doesn't know what's killing her, doesn't know fucking anything that's going on. All he can do is watch as a mother seizes, until her body stops, stills, and her belly inflates until bursting like a blooming flower. A plume of gray erupts into the non-air. Jay's eyes widen, inhaling—old books, tobacco, mothballs, a tinge of lilac—as her eyes glass over. Unseeing, yet

"Open it!" Ashleigh shouts from inside the house, her voice traveling from the open window on the second story. The front

door creaks when opened. Inside smells of disinfectant and the unmistakable aroma of an abandoned home. It's heartbreaking to see his sister's house like this, especially when she cared so much about it only a little while ago. He shuts the door when Nicole comes in.

"Where you at?" he calls. Nicole stands nearby, quiet. The entry lights don't work. The kitchen down the hall and the living room to the right are cavernous, only broken by dimming afternoon light breaking through the heavy curtains, revealing a dust coating.

"I swear I paid the electric," he mutters to his wife. "But... I don't know if it was that or the rent. With work, I'm—I can't..."

"It's fine, Jay." She rests her hand on his arm. "You can't do everything."

"But she's my—"

"Where do you think?" Ashleigh shouts.

Of course, how stupid of him. Keeping their shoes on, they take the stairs, avoiding yellowed books and newspapers stacked by the banister. The jaundiced wallpaper uncurls near the dirty baseboards, revealing darkly spotted blue paint. Could be mold, could be something else. Jay reminds himself he needs to come back soon to clean up if all fails.

Upstairs, three doors stand open.

"Don't look in the other rooms, you'll only get more grossed out," he says. "Keep your eyes on my back, okay?"

She nods.

They hurry down the hall to the master bedroom.

"What brings you two here?" Ashleigh says as he opens the door.

Old clothes, washed or not, pile against the box spring and dresser; crystal ashtrays are scattered haphazardly; dregs of cigarettes and empty packs still linger, left from before the diag-

noses; magazines and more books poke out from underneath the bed frame. The flat screen TV on the dresser's muted, the news on.

"Do I need a reason to see my sister?"

She gives a long sigh. "You two look nice. Did you drive or fly?"

Turning away, coughing, he shakes his head. *What the hell was that? How is this shit getting in?* He goes to rub his eyes but smudges the visor.

"What happened?" Crews breaks through the silence. "Why the *fuck* did you ignore me?"

He almost talks about the memory, seemingly triggered by the dust, but stops himself, saying, "Found Kat, the pregnant crew member."

"Oh."

"She told me what she could." He wipes his visor clear. "But... she died soon after that."

Crews doesn't speak for a moment, then: "Sorry that happened. From what I remember, she was a nice gal."

The thing she had thrown at him is tucked between the wall and a container. He retrieves it, flicking away not-yet-hardened goo. "Yeah," he says. The end's mushroom tipped, a yellow ring dimly glowing around the base. Jay quietly makes his way back through the narrow passageways into the main portion of the Bay. The weight of Kat's passing is heavy on his shoulders; the loss of a baby, despite what spilled from her groin not resembling anything human, weighs even heavier.

What was she trying to say? 'Eco-something' and 'Would get out.' What does that mean? He pushes the thoughts aside, not caring what it means since he can't figure it out on his own anyway. What mattered was that a person had died in front of him, and he couldn't do anything to save her. He was useless, a bystander to a death that likely caused more pain than he could know. Even after hundreds of years since being a detective, it still hit him as though it was his first. No one deserved what happened to Kat and her baby.

Keep focused. Mourn later.

In the open again, he glances over the containers. He again notices the circular protrusions, the ring of red lights around their middle. Holds the rod up...

Oh.

It's a key.

He turns to the giant door leading into the outside, his attention pulled to the box with WASTE burnt onto its side.

If it's nearest to the door, then it's likely the most recent shipment. Earlier ones pushed deeper into storage. If that's true, then that's probably the match that lit the wick.

Its lock on top is scratched to hell as though whoever tried to seal it did it frantically, blindly. Reminds him of car ignitions, white marks all over from the key. Jay rotates the rod around and, holding it vertically, slowly guides it into the center.

The red lights turn green, and the yellow on the key does the same. The top of the box splits into fours and recedes—

Shit or something as foul smacks him when it erupts from inside. "Fuck!" Jay stumbles back, dropping the key, backhanding the gunk from his visor, and draws his weapon.

"What?" Crews shouts "What happened?

"Jay?"

Breathing heavy, he aims at, near, above the box. The ceiling—

Two sets of elongated, knobby talon prints scurry up the wall and vanish into the solidified pitch hanging from the ceiling.

"Jay! What the hell happened?" Crews's words fast, loud, but deaf in Jay's ears.

Pointing the weapon at the pile of remains, he slowly backs to the closest wall. Until now he hasn't realized the aroma—warm honey, maple, flowers—clawing at his non-existent glands in the non-existent air. Even the taste buds he was told he didn't have are singing with caramelized sugar. It should smell like shit. Like death. Like bodies and decay and whatever-the-fuck in the box, but it's like he's in a damn bakery, a candy store.

"If you don't fuckin' answer me, you—"

Jay scans the prints again.

"Shut up for a minute," he spits. The mic goes dead.

They look... sort of human.

The five talons look like widely-spaced toes, but malformed, clearly, and stretched out...

If they were shorter... And the shape...

Clicking sounds come from behind then above. Jay holds his breath. No, not clicking; it's *chittering.*

"Get out, Jay, get the fuck out of there, *now.*"

Aiming his weapon at the ceiling, Jay sees a flash of gray streak past. Thick drops of filth crash onto the containers and floor, like wet paint slapping steel. Jay gives chase, rushing between shipments, keeping his gun pointed upward without falling or running into something.

"Jay? You listening to me? Get the fuck out of there."

He pivots around the corner leading back to the entrance of the Main Hall. The barrel shivers in his trembling hand. Keeping to the wall, he sidesteps to the door, one hand behind him searching, finding the knob. It opens and he steps out, and he slams against the wall while pushing the door closed.

Jay hunkers, weapon in both hands by his face, breathing heavy, waiting...

"You still alive? Answer me."

After a few beats, he crab walks away, and when the floor rises, he stands and hurries.

"Get me off this damn ship," he says. "I have a good damn idea what happened to the crew, the ship; it doesn't matter what it is."

"Hold on, Jay—"

"No. It's some type of disease. An infection. Something that fucking *kills* people. Picked it up wherever. Now you know, you can send more people in. I don't care. Just get me out."

"Jay—"

"No. Better, fucking nuke this ship. Have it self-destruct. Start over."

"Will you listen for one damn minute?" Crews roars.

Despite the vitriol surging from his mouth, Jay quiets. Making it to the higher floor, he beelines for the airlock.

"You can't get sick, you don't have an immune system, antibodies, that whole shit. And you can't die, remember?"

"I can, and I can. This might not be my body or my insides, but I can sure as shit still die. Might not be *real* death but still death, and I don't want it. Not again."

"True, but even so, it'll be painless. You won't feel a thing. HUSK's override that, if worse comes to worse. Hell, you might even enjoy it. And after, you'll be rebooted into another body back home."

"The Moon's not my home, space isn't my home; nowhere's my fucking home anymore. Everyone I knew and loved is long gone." His heart pummels his chest. Lungs flutter, desperately trying to catch his breath. "I don't know why you're trying to convince me to stay when I've done my job." Through the door, the airlock is dimly lit by long lights along the ceiling. The barrier still missing. "You and I know enough to figure out what happened here. The job's done, Crews. Get. Me. Out."

"Look," he says flatly. "I'm not taking you from the *Candlewood.*"

Jay halts before the sealed door leading to the connector.

"Wh—why the hell not?"

"There's a whole list of them, but the one that matters the most is that I'm your fucking boss, and the job isn't done until I say it is."

His eyes widen, and his grip tightens over the pistol. Teeth clench. "Are you serious?"

"Another is that if it is a disease," he continues, ignoring him, "an infection, you also may be infected, or at least a carrier."

"No, that's impossible. You just said I can't get sick, no real parts to carry a disease."

"It could be something we don't know, something HUSKs can carry."

"But I haven't touched a fucking thing, and when I did, it was under *your* direct orders." Jay recalls the floral scents, the sugary tastes cloying at his throat, the incomplete memories of his wife and sister. Doesn't say a damn word. Living, getting off this ship, is paramount.

"It doesn't matter who said or did what, and whatever this disease is sounds severe, strong, and I don't know anything about it. You could be a carrier even just being around it."

"Bullshit, Crews. Quarantine me then; put me in the airlock or a container for a couple days. There're ways to keep everyone safe."

"No way am I risking it, Jay."

"You fucking put me here," Jay seethes. "Now get me off."

"*No.*"

Jay chucks the weapon across the room and grips the neck of his suit. He wants to rip it off. Wants his flesh to feel real air, wants to be free and no longer imprisoned by the suit or the ship or the oppressive, endless emptiness surrounding everything. He screams unintelligible words as he punches a locker. A dull pain shoots up his arm. There's no sound, and he longs for that too. For things to be real, to be normal.

Leaning his head against a wall, he says, "Crews?"

No answer.

"Answer me, jackass."

"Can't."

"Can't? Why not?"

"Bit busy—*shit*!"

Jay pushes off the wall. "What happened? What's going on?"

Silence.

"Drift."

"What about it?"

"I hadn't—*damnit*—calculated the planetary drift properly. The pull of Jupiter is stronger than I realized. Remember when I said I wasn't a pilot?"

"What's that mean?"

"Means I'm being dragged away from the ship, and even if I wanted to get you out, I couldn't. If you opened the airlock, you'd free drift until your air ran out before I could get you."

Although his insides aren't real, he feels his gut plummet. A clamminess rolls over him, and rage bubbles in the pit of his stomach. Crews's trying to cover his ass, trying to make it seem like there are real reasons for Jay to stay on the ship, but he's the one fucking up. Is there a disease, an infection? Is he lying about the drift too? He couldn't be, because why would he lie about that? He's paying Jay to find out what happened, and he doesn't seem like the type who likes blowing money.

"Wouldn't this ship be moving too?"

"Apparently not; it's right outside of the drift. *Fuck*!"

"How long will it take to be back in range?"

"Twenty-four hours at the most. Can't rush it or I'll kill us both."

"What if I drive this ship? Move it closer."

"Don't be a fucking idiot, Jay. You've never flown a ship, let alone one in space."

He runs his hand over his helmet. "What the hell am I supposed to do then?"

"Don't die and waste my down payment."

Metal clangs against metal, echoing from the ship's bowels. Nails on steel; click, click, click.

How is it making noise without air?

"Fuck you, Crews," he says, and mutes the intercom.

Fine, fine, fine.

Jay snatches his firearm from the floor, sticking it to his waist, and rushes from the airlock, across the Main Hall, and into the Mess. More clanging in distance, sharp nails chattering against the honeycombed floor. Jay nearly trips barreling through the debris, into the beds, then past into the closet.

The door slides closed behind him.

He quickly empties out a lower trunk—clothes, food, a tablet that won't power on—then lying on the ground, shimmies his way inside it. It's tight, but with his knees to his chest, Jay manages to fit. The front lid doesn't close. He's a little glad, afraid that if it did it wouldn't open again.

The overhead lights turn off a few moments later.

Click, click, click.

Jay holds his breath and slides his weapon from his waist, holding it in front of his knees. Temples hammering. His wide eyes sting without sweat.

Click, click, click.

Curtains move.

Oh shit.

The door glides open, light falling in before the overheads kick back on. He clenches his teeth, pressing his tongue to the roof of his mouth. Only the thing's head comes through the doorway, if it could be considered a head at all. Four indented crevices from opposing directions converge in the center of an almond-shaped skull. Shallow pockets and craters of varying size cover the umber, hardened flesh. Everything slathered in grease. Thick ichor drips from the seams, puddling and congealing on the floor.

It has no mouth, but it seems to huff all the same, the aroma of sugar and spices wafting over him.

Do I shoot it?

Do I pray and hope the gods of the future save my ass?

It doesn't move. Doesn't look around. Does nothing but remain still. Heavy silence weighs over Jay, and his legs and arms are cramping. It recedes from the doorway, and the door closes. Its talons clicking on the floor dwindle until Jay can no longer hear them. The lights wink off.

When Jay releases his breath.

Jay can't remember feeling like this in his past life, but he's sure he wasn't. In his line of work, he saw a lot of abhorrent things, and if he broke down each time he came across them, he wouldn't have been able to do his job. He imagines he bottled them up, pushed them down; if they weren't breaking the surface, he could keep going.

Do emotions not carry over, new ones coming with the HUSK? I've never been this afraid before, this... defenseless. But I can't stay here forever. If that thing finds me here, I'm fucked. I need to move.

It takes him a while to calm, to mentally prepare for what could potentially happen, then he crawls out from the trunk. Weapon raised, he creeps back into the hall. Dotted black trickles across the floor, some smearing the pulled back curtains. In the Mess, stains, food packets and stools and other odds-and-ends blanket the ground. Before leaving, Jay switches the short-wave on.

"Just to let you know, I'm not dead," he whispers. "But I'm killing the comm until I can figure this out."

Short-wave off.

When he was alive, the method Jay used to figure out a case was by running headfirst, endlessly searching, investigating, interviewing, on and on until exhaustion took him to the nearest couch or cot. He didn't wait and see like some others. Staying put was wasting the victim's time. His body a vessel to carry him to the next break in the case, the next clue leading him to the perpetrator. But now, the last place Jay wants to go is through the doorway. His feet leaden.

Has the HUSK changed who I was—am too? Must've.

It feels more *right* to stay put, to remain here, to allow his mind to unravel a plan instead of rushing it. He yearns for a pen and paper, something to create and see what is ahead of him.

At a glance, he doesn't find anything worthwhile, and he doesn't want to sift through garbage. He lifts and uprights a toppled over stool by the upturned table. Its legs hum before magnetically connecting to the floor.

Slapping his weapon to his waist, he sits.

Fine. We'll do it this new way.

There are several bodies: the mechanic, the nurse, the 'passengers,' and Kat. The ship only has a handful of rooms, excluding the shipment room. Jay opens the APC to go over the ship's map. It seems to him that whatever the monster is, it started in the Captain's Quarters: the darkness, the flittering soot, the barrier sectioning off the room. It's like a cocoon, in a way. It must've formed—grew?—there and attacked the crew from bow to stern until Kat was able to put it—back?—into the container. What the black stuff is, Jay hasn't the faintest clue. Could be something organic, alive like plants. Or if Crews is right, a virus or parasite.

Jay sighs, reaches to rub his eyes, halts.

"Ugh..."

He has twenty-six hours at most to survive assuming nothing goes wrong and he doesn't use more air than expected. Will Crews still retrieve him if the monster's still alive? Would he jeopardize his own life for Jay's?

Probably not.

"So that means it has to be killed or contained," he mutters. He raises his weapon, turning it in his hand. *Can it even die? Have things changed that much in the future that even death is questionable?*

"No, no." He shakes his head, uncertain if the gun *could* kill something like it. The better option is to hide and wait. If it attacks him, he'll defend himself the best he can, but Jay decides he's not going to hunt it down. It may not be his body, but he doesn't want to be in pain or die, even if it's a false death.

Sifting through his memories of the rooms he has visited, the safest one seems to be the Pilot's. One door, no exits. There he has the monitors to keep track of it and the ship's functionality, the little good it does. It's better to have it than not. He'll have to barricade the door so he can rest, but doesn't remember if the chairs in the room were movable. If they're not, he guesses he just won't get much rest.

Jay double-checks the gun's ammo. All twelve slanted lights are illuminated yellow. It's not many, but may be enough.

Wonder if there's more ammo on board...

71

VI

26:47:03

I N THE MAIN HALL, he glances down both ends. No monster, no sound of it either. It's unsettling it *can* make sounds without air, *can* create scents he shouldn't be able to smell. Jay wonders what else it can do that it's not meant to.

Back to the plan, Jay.

He nods and makes for the front of the *Candlewood*, checking over his shoulder every few seconds.

The Pilot's door slides shut behind him, but he still checks to ensure it's secure. The room's the same as it was when he left it initially—pilot chairs, another chair in front of a bay of security monitors in the corner, a center console of buttons, switches, keyboards, and a flat screen... But the windshield seems... off.

Jay gets on top of a chair, places his hands onto the console's top, and leans toward the upper right corner of the glass. He can't completely discern it from the space beyond, but there's definitely something there.

Headlights on.

The glass ripples like oil, a holographic gleam...

Shit.

The outer hull must be covered too. He imagines it's entering or exiting through captain's place . It coalesces across the glass like rapid frost, slow yet fast enough for Jay to watch in real time, fanning over and out like water from a leak. It wasn't doing this before. It's *alive* now... *Or it might have always been, only resting.*

The glass will be covered soon, meaning the entire ship will eventually be too. This means Jay won't be able to leave; the exit will be sealed by gunk.

"Crews," he says, then realizes the intercom's off. Turns it on. "Crews."

"Oh, now you wanna talk?"

"There's another problem."

"That's not terrible," Crews says. "If that shit scrapes away with your finger, then you shouldn't have a hard time breaking a hole through the outer hull."

"And if the stuff outside is thicker or denser?"

Silence, then, "We'll figure it out if the time comes."

As much as I hate it, he's right. No use worrying about something I can't change right now.

The pilot's chair swivels under Jay, and he carefully gets down. Hunkering, he inspects its base. Wide bolts protrude along a stand sloping into the floor. Jay grips the base and shakes it, but there's no give; it doesn't even budge. The other chair's the same.

"Well shit."

Straightening, he scans the room another time. Nothing's movable—not the center console, not the bay of screens, not the third chair in front of him.

"Can I lock the door with the computer?" he says.

"Probably," Crews says, "but your guess is as good as mine

on how to do that. Don't do programming and don't know ship commands besides the ones I gave you."

Of course you don't. What do you actually do besides sit on your ass and collect a check?

Jay hovers by the keyboard, fingers ready, but fear and hesitation swell in the back of his mind. He doesn't want to fuck anything up, doesn't want to make matters worse by poking and prodding the ship's computer. Dropping his hands, he turns and goes to the monitors.

Most that weren't covered before now are. He can no longer view most of the front-end rooms nor any external cameras lining the *Candlewood*. The Engine's cam is smudged, but the one in the Pilot's Room is fine, and the Cargo Bay can partially be made out, not any worse or better. All the others are dead. Flying blinder than ever before.

Whatever the creature is, it's being intentional... smart... *sentient*.

Jay sighs. It's unreliable to go by memory and the APC map. There's only so much a 3-D grid can do, and his memory has been shot from the get—

All the cams in the Shipment Bay are suddenly completely blotted by black. Moments later, the Engine's meets the same fate. They black out, one after another, until the last cam working is in the Pilot's Room. Jay stares at himself staring at himself, terrified.

Facing the door, he raises his weapon, backing to the center of the room, his eyes wild, wide. Blood or something like it rampaging through his artificial veins. Either the HUSK has adrenaline or his mind is slipping too. Or maybe both.

"Crews."

"What?"

"Big chance this job won't get done."

"Why?"

"Thing's coming for me—or this room—I don't know. It's smart."

"Why would it do that? Why would it want that room, or you?"

"I don't fucking know," he spits. "Why don't you come on board and ask?"

"Use the gun. No matter whatever the hell it is, it can't survive EBs."

Doesn't bother asking what those are. Something Bullets. "And if it does?"

He chuckles. "Jay, we both know the answer to that."

He puts the barrel ahead, legs wide and locked, shoulders back, core clenched. Deja vu washes over him. It's like the old days when things went too wild and he had to resort to using deadly force.

It'll be fine.

It'll be okay.

You'll get through this.

The door slides open revealing a maw of nothingness. An external layer of solidified soot coats every surface the overhead lights touch and the surfaces they don't. Jay stands at the end of the world in the last remaining light at the end of an empty tunnel. Lead blankets him, a heaviness gathering on his shoulders, like piling cement. His hands tremble.

The creature erupts from the dark, lunging into the room from the hall's ceiling. It crawls overhead, weaving like water, toward the windshield. Jay pulls the trigger again and again. Yellow bullets go wide, charring the metal. Nothing like firing a real gun. It's lighter and stronger.

Its pocketed body elongates and bends with malleable bones stretching and retracting in a comb pattern, avoiding every one of Jay's shots. What he does hit is the hull, the holes quickly sealing by the creature's discharge. Reaching the windshield, it drops, spinning mid-air, and lands, perching on the console.

Jay rushes back, gun pointed. Three, maybe two, bullets are left; he's too terrified to confirm. It lurches for him, its long body condensing into a narrow shape, its meaty talons placed forefront. Jay shoots too early, missing. He drops onto his back, aiming up, and uses the last two EBs. One misses by an inch; the last connects, ricocheting off its scalp. Flecks of burnt bone spray the air before colorless fluid splashes the ceiling and his helmet. Doesn't seem like it hit anything vital, yet it collapses to the floor as he rolls away.

He jumps to his feet, backpedaling through the doorway, holding the empty firearm in front of him as though it'll do anything.

The creature's still, like a slumbering dog. Before, it was too fast to catch its details, but now... Tufts of blonde hair sprout from the gray bone running down its spine and underbelly, both parts muscley, slick, bulbous, made up by what seems like... *organs*; a nose juts from craters along one side, what looks like earlobes and teeth from the other, nubs of pink and pale flesh sporadically sprouting like weeds... The almond-shaped end rattles. The four connecting seams severe and fall back, loose tar webbing pulled apart revealing an inner, translucent shell coming undone. An emerald tendril or root or vine, splotched with hints of teal, protrudes and rises, sprouting out and over the creature. It splinters at the top, peeling back into four petals, revealing a cerulean stigma outlined by turquoise, bioluminescent beads.

What the fuck is that?

Each bead, one following another, pulsates.

He hears a lilting sound, a soft alarm like a bell tower ringing far over the horizon. So faint Jay believes it's not even there, that it's only his mind because something so innocent and pure sounding couldn't possibly be coming from the monstrosity on the ground.

He shakes his head. It doesn't matter where it's coming from. But he still doesn't move, doesn't break eye contact. Apparently finished, the beads dim, the green petals fold over the stigma, and the tendril retracts into the body. The see-through coating returns, and treacle webs from the almond edges come together and pull its head closed, sealing. Not a hint of what just occurred remains.

The crudely bent legs tremble, its body jolting as though it's zapped by electricity.

No way to defend himself, no way to deal with what's returning to the living or waking up, Jay slaps the gun to his waist, spins, and books it into the nothingness.

"Is there ammo anywhere on this ship?" Jay spits.

"Might be some in the Cap's room. No weaponry was allowed on the ship for safety precaution. Too many Hoppers coming on board to let anyone have a gun."

"Great," he says.

The darkness is absolute beyond the light. What weak light there was is now gone. Even with Jay's lights, he can only make out a few inches in front of him, as though the oppressive gloom devours his futile attempts of visibility. His fists vanish in the black with every swing as he pumps his legs faster. The Captain's Quarters are near, Jay remembers, but it feels like he's been running for miles, as if the hall goes on infinitely.

A quick glance over his shoulder, the Pilot's Bar's a faint speck like a star in space. He slows enough to continue running and to be able to open the APC. Going by the ship's grid, and if he's right, the room should be on his left.

When he turns, the Pilot's Room winks out of existence, but

straight ahead he finds the branching walkway leading to the Captain's Quarters. The door's still open, sludge still seeping and oozing over the floor.

Inside, the wall remains. Jay rakes enough away with his fingers to squeeze through. On the other side, he immediately feels lighter, his body ascending with the scattershot vacuum above. His lights didn't work well here before, but compared to the outside, they're a godsend now. They reveal a bed against the far wall, a storage cabinet tucked in the upper left corner, and a square stand or console beside the bed... *Doesn't have his own bathroom. That sucks.* Beside Jay, pushed between the barrier and normal wall, is a bone-riddled explosion of a corpse. White pieces speckle the frozen black. The pointed ends break off little by little, turning to dust and drifting toward the punctured ceiling.

Jay tears open the cabinet. No bullets or magazines or boxes of ammo, but there's an APC in the back behind a banded stack of hydration and empty foil wrappers. *Guess the captain wasn't one for sentimental things.* The APC's not loaded with an MLID, though. Jay moves around the bed to the stand/console. Steel gray slivers appear through the coating. *Looks heavy.*

Crouching, he scrapes away the dark exterior to find a small, inlaid screen. Touching it brings it to life with a green electronic light. White text reads: INPUT YOUR FOUR-DIGIT PIN

"Would you know what Cap's PIN would be?"

"Uh... No. Only met him a few times, so we weren't chums. He was a big history nerd."

"What kind of history?"

"Oddly, just his own. His family tree, his ancestors, that sort of thing. He knew all their names, birthdays, death dates, etc. Hey—wait—I remember him going on about his family beginning or migrating or something in 1723. Went on about it for fucking hours the first time I met him. Give that a go."

Jay does, and the white text turns into a green checkmark. The front pops open, sending flecks into the air.

"Shit, it worked."

"Don't mention it."

Lined in dark velvet, the goo hasn't reached inside. There's a weapon similar to Jay's on the shelf over a wide space beneath, except this one is darker and has gray stripes down the barrel with white in-between. He sets aside his empty firearm and takes the new one. The grip's solid but malleable, forming to his palm. At the safe's bottom is what looks like an ammo clip, curved and rectangular but much lighter. He tilts the gun forward and the clip smoothly slides up the handle, as though greased. He imagines a satisfying click even though there isn't one.

Twelve dim, green lights on its side illuminate, casting a misty glow. Putting the firearm to his hip, Jay checks the locker again and finds a holograph photo in the back.

Clip must've been blocking it.

He holds it close to his visor.

Must've been his family.

Within the plastic card-shaped object, a blonde-haired man with crow's feet around light blue eyes and a young man's smile has a thin woman tucked under his arm. She has wide, green eyes, her hair matches the man's, and her mouth's open in a gasp. Two little boys poke up from the bottom of the photo, both blonde. One has his eyes squeezed shut, a big smile on his face; the other is laughing and clenching his small hands.

Flipping it around, Jay finds a MLID taped to its back. He peels it off and puts the photo back gently as though not wanting to be discovered for stealing. He closes the door and it pressure seals.

Popping out the nurse's MLID and setting it aside, he puts the new one in.

I'll listen when it's somewhat safe.

As he straightens, he gives another glance around the room. More sludge grows into the inside of the hanging cabinet, and when he moves, Jay realizes it was doing the same to his boots. Inching up his ankles, it snaps and leaves a wound on the floor. Jay has to tear a new hole through the wall before he can leave.

Listening, he hears nothing. Palpable silence fills the non-existent air. The gloam thickened, somehow deeper, darker than the substance covering the ship. He doesn't know where to go, where to hide. The *Candlewood* seemed bigger when he arrived but now it's closing in on him, shrinking. No corners or nooks to shove himself into, no rooms to bar himself in, just an encroaching emptiness matching the one growing in Jay's mind.

His thoughts drift to his suicide, what he must've felt leading up to it, still unsure why he committed such an act. The memories he experiences here are the only ones he can recall, assumingly a by-product of the ash. Jay wishes he could remember more, suddenly wanting it more than he wants to survive this job, uncertain if he'll have the chance to recollect anything else. A yearning overtakes him. Turning and stepping back through the wall, he crouches at the imploded crew member's corpse.

I can't believe I'm doing this. It's fucking stupid, but I have to know.

He grabs a handful of the putty between two pockets of bristling bone, oozing between his fingers. Double-checks the tar partition to find it's resealed. Leaning in, he tears it from the body. A puff of dust breathes over him, and the reek of tobacco, the faint smell of coming rain smacks. . .

Jay, hands in his pockets, stands by his wife, who sits on the edge of the bed, her hands clasped on her lap. His sister's greasy, frayed, blonde hair tied back in a tail, her white t-shirt stained by something red and yellow.

"How's it been?" he says.

Ashleigh waves her hand in the air. "Oh, you know, perfect as usual."

He nods, rocks on his heels, unsure why they came in the first place. Talking to his sister has always been like pulling teeth, or at least when the two of them talk. "So..."

"You got the report?" she cuts in.

"Yes," Nicole says before Jay can. "Dr. Snoyer faxed us your papers last week."

"Thought so." She looks at the open window, dark clouds gathering beyond. She grins. "Is that why you came? Guilt?"

"No," he firmly says. "We came because we love you and want you to come live with us in PA. You shouldn't be here alone, shouldn't be living like this now that—"

Her glare burns into him, hazel eyes fierce. "That I'm dying? Well, I've been living alone, like this, since the diagnosis, so why shouldn't I stay that way? You've been paying my bills, so now—what?—you think you can rescue me too? No thanks."

All the air in the room is sucked out through the open window. Jay looks to his wife, gnawing on her bottom lip and looking at her fingers gripping her dress. His phone buzzes in his pocket. He clenches it in his sweaty palm.

"If you won't come live with us," he says, "you could at least seek treatment, try to beat it."

Ashleigh shakes her head, coughs into her arm. "Are you an idiot? It's stage four, there's no helping that." Tears well under her furrowed eyes. "I'm not dying bald and decrepit, looking like I feel. I'm going on my own terms, not yours or the doctor's."

Outside a storm brews, thunder rattling the house. A splatter of rain hits in the pane.

He clenches his teeth; the cell phone digs into his tightening fist. Heat rises from his gut. "So, what? You're just going to lie there and die because 'it's on your own terms?' What kind of bull—"

Nicole shoots up, grabs his arms. "Jay, she's sick."

"Sick or not, she's being a stubborn dumbass," he spits around his wife's head. "I'm offering you a chance to be around the last family you got, expenses paid, but you'd rather die in this dump?"

"Yeah," Ashleigh says, eyes red-rimmed. "Yeah, I'd rather fucking die here than take charity from my little brother. Mom and Dad might've taken it, but not me, Jason. I've been fine on my own for fifteen years, I'll be fine on my own now."

"And when you can't breathe?" he roars. "Can't walk? Can't get out of the bed to piss? What then? You're going to just wallow in your filth because you're too proud to accept help?"

"Jay, that's enough," Nicole spits in his ear. "It's her decision. It's her life."

He turns away and stomps to the door. "Whatever, fine. Let her live her life the way she wants." Mutters in the hall, "What little she has left."

"Fuck." He reels back, shellshocked, dumbfounded, falling onto his ass as though he's wrenched out of water. He doesn't have time to go over what he discovered; scratching comes from the other side of the barrier. Must've not heard the creature coming into the room during the memory.

Jay scrambles to his feet, wiping the dust from his visor, and searches frantically for somewhere to hide, finding nowhere. Shoving himself in the opposite corner, he squeezes his body into a ball. Firearm held off to the side, he watches over his knees as the wall gives way.

The tip of the almond-shaped head slips through as though

that's all it requires to see, to feel out the space. Jay holds his breath. Not enough of it shown to risk shooting, and if he doesn't kill it with the first shot, he's sure he won't have the chance to pop off another.

Second by palpable second, nothing happens. It remains still, unmoving. Jay's heart's wild against his chest, the feel of adrenaline flooding his false veins, preparing for action. Muscles clench. Joints tense. The reasons it cannot see him are beyond him. Maybe its eyes or whatever it uses to see are further back on its head? Maybe it can't see but senses vibrations, temperatures, or some form of energy he cannot possibly fathom? Either way, it doesn't matter much for its head retracts through the wall, and the clicking of talons fades away.

Jay doesn't move until the hole seals.

What the hell was that?

Minutes later, when all's quiet, he stands and scratches a hole in the wall and peeks through. Nothing. Silence.

It's impossible to keep safe while it's alive. Maybe there's something in that box that could help me kill it? Or, I don't know, trap it? Plus, if it's smart, I doubt it'll return to the place it was trapped in so soon. He slowly widens the gap to pass through. *There's only one way to test that theory.*

VII

T HE ROOMS HE HURRIES past are like the last. Flaky barriers fill doorways, a moving, growing black. Every passing
moment is another he looks over his shoulder, at the ceiling.
He feels eyes on him from everywhere but finds nothing, no
one. When the floor declines, he knows he's going in the right
direction. At the bottom, he comes to the Cargo Bay door, still
open. Sludge plasters the inside of the doorframe, forming tiny
stalactites above, and crawls up the wall and huge garage door.

He immediately cuts left upon entering, through a crooked
aisle, and between a container catty-corner to the wall is a small
cubby where he huddles. Extinguishes his light.

Waits.

He scans his surroundings. Only one way through, except
from above. Something metallic with a red light glints by the
wall. It takes him a moment to remember... *The key. Must've
thrown it by mistake when the thing came out of the box. I'm
not risking it yet.*

His thoughts turn to the memory, questions sprouting from
them.

*I had a sister, and she was sick. I treated her so badly... Why
would I do that? I'm not like that... Am I? Are these memories*

even right, or are they fucked up from the dust or from being a HUSK or from—I don't know. I don't think I could be that cold to someone, especially someone sick.

Jay wants to ask Crews if what he's remembering is true or altered in some way... But revealing that the ship's affecting his mind may lead to Crews not retrieving him, abandoning him because he's likely infected.

Focus on the task at hand, Jay. He listens intently, the near absolute darkness surrounding him. There're no sounds, no indication of anything alive but his breathing for what feels like an hour... Believing it's safe, he lifts his arm and carefully opens the APC.

I know I shouldn't watch it now, but will I have a better chance later? Probably not.

Jay presses a button on the screen's side, and it illuminates. He remembers Crews telling him about the cap having a V-MLID, but he's still surprised when a video appears on screen, overtaking the 3-D grid of the ship.

A man fidgets with what must be his APC, adjusting it and setting it down in front of him. There's no audio, which is weird. Might've been corrupted or damaged with the ship. Either way, Jay's thankful for it. The room the man's in is bare except for a cabinet tucked into the corner of the ceiling and the bed he's sitting on.

Centered now, the captain says, subtitles reading, "Ah, okay, here we go."

He's middle-aged, has brown eyes with crow's feet, and short, blonde hair. Wrinkled jowls and a furrowed brow. Military, Jay guesses. He's wearing an umber jumpsuit zipped up to his chin. *Must be the crew's work uniforms; they're not much different than mine.*

He sighs before continuing. "I don't know where to begin."

Raises his hands, lets them fall. "Don't know how much time's left." He looks away from the camera then back, scratches his cheek. "We procured a shipment from Triton at 04:30. Routine pick-up. Nothing weird. We've used IPTS on Triton more times than I can count. Hell, most of the crew know the movers there on a first-name basis.

"So we didn't think anything of it. Why would it be any different? Anyone would've done it in my—*our* position. And who ships something like that through regular interplanetary transit, honestly?

"Anyway, we do checks on everything, don't want to take any chances on illegal shipments." He runs a hand through his hair. "But we were in a hurry—fucking Mike—and were behind on a different shipment. So we didn't do the check right away, no big deal, really. Happens sometimes, plus we're familiar with the shipments we get through IPTS—construction material, substances for repurposing, etc.—and the people we deal with. It's as above board as it can be."

Tears form in his eyes. He sniffles, wipes his nose with the back of his hand. "I'm getting off track. So, we leave Triton on a direct course to Enceladus to deliver the shipment. Fifteen-day trip at most, without stops. Fifteen hours later, twenty at most, we finally do the checks. Nothing out of the ordinary until Kat checks a small container. Right from the start, it's strange that someone paid to have something that small shipped through IPTS. It seems like it'd be personal, a gift delivery, something that'd go through IPPS. We usually get massive things in bulk from businesses... Kat runs it through the database; no tags, no information, no codes. Never was logged into their or our system before shipment.

"The lock was scratched to all hell, as if someone rushed to seal it before getting it sent out." He exhales, puts his face in his hands. Tar stains the tips of his fingers, inky veins run beneath his fingernails, fading into pale skin. "So Kat pings me. Unidentifiable shipments do happen sometimes, but she said this one *felt* wrong and didn't want to make any mistakes. This happens to everyone once in a while; people want the responsibility taken off their hands, just in case. Saw it *a ton* in the service.

"I go down there, and she gives me the key. I do a once over—walk around it, look at the top, bottom—but there's nothing special about it. Kat stands next to me while I unlock it, and there's just..." He chuckles. "*Shit*. Actual diarrhea. It looks and smells like it, and we all assume that's what it is. A waste container. See it sometimes, but typically the IPWM takes them. Must've been a mix-up, or some jackass trying to play a prank." The captain shakes his head. "No matter what it is, I have to do a manual inspection, make sure nothing's hiding in there, like a bomb. I ping Cathy to bring down some extra-length medical gloves. Mike comes in a couple minutes later carrying them. Tells me he was on the way to see the '*shit-ment*' and grabbed them from her along the way.

"Gloves on up to my elbows, I shove my hands deep into the filth. At first, I felt nothing but swampy water and floating chunks of God knows what. It was like rummaging in a septic tank back on Earth. Then—then I feel something rocky, jagged around the edges, in the corners. All one piece, connecting to four segments leading to something oval-shaped in the middle. Ridges down its sides, opposite of the four branching parts. It felt..." He looks down. "*Floral*, almost. Like a real flower petal, but... *not?* I can't really explain it better than that. I touch the oval's narrow top, and something bites my fingers, or I cut them on something. All five at once. I didn't feel anything alive swimming in there, anything with teeth or claws or sharp nails, just the shit and whatever was underneath. I rip my hand out, screaming, splashing filth everywhere, and tear the glove off."

He blinks back tears.

"I *felt* being bitten, I know I did. But when I looked at my damn hand, there weren't any markings or scratches. No cuts or bruises or blood. There were these... these little dots under my fingernails, like puncture wounds, like moles. I can't remember if they were there before or after, and I'm questioning myself when Kat and Mike come to help me, but I stop them. Put on a stern face and tell them I'm fine, everything's fine.

"I tell them to seal the container, nothing to worry about. They calm down, and Kat marks the container as WASTE. I didn't want to, but I know if I didn't go get a work-up, I'd be forced to eventually by Cathy." He rolls his eyes. "Always one wanting to *make sure* we're healthy and stable. So I go there after, and she checks me out. Everything's A-OK. Healthy as an ox. I didn't bring up the finger markings since my readings were in the green. With a good bill of health, I return to my quarters. Alan tried to talk to me on the way back, but I got a massive headache and didn't want to entertain him."

Facing the camera, he's glaring. "But Cathy was wrong—I was wrong. Something's inside me. I can *feel* it." He raises his hand, looks at it as though it's not his. "Running through my veins, digging into muscle, burrowing into my organs. I don't know what to do. I can't tell the crew what's happening, especially after being told I was fine. They'll think I'm just another crackpot, and I don't need them not trusting my judgment..." The captain sighs. "Have to hold out until I can get a full work-up at a hospital. We're mid-trip, so it's useless to contact anyone right now. It'll take less time for us to travel to Enceladus than for them to send someone out to the *Candlewood*."

The captain quiets, stills. Jay believes the video's frozen until he continues.

"Shouldn't have opened that damn box. Now we need help, because whatever's inside me is working fast." The APC is lifted and brought in close to the man's face. Jay believed initially it was only crow's feet around the eyes, but they're not wrinkles. Black cracks are spreading, webbing out from his eyes. Blue irises fissured with the same, splintering at the corneas. Subtly, they move, pulse like veins. "See that? It's not me, right? I'm not going insane, am I?" He puts the APC back down. "Hoping the docs will be able to help—have some idea of what the hell's going on, or at least... I don't know... Stop it before it gets any worse, because I feel and look like shit, and I can't imagine what it'll be like by the time they see me.

"Shit—memory running low." He reaches toward the camera. "Captain Fox signing off."

———————

Jay closes the APC. His arms feel heavy. Palpable silence weighs over him.

That's what happened, what kicked this off. Cap shoved his hand in some shit and got sick...

Info doesn't help me now, since I still don't know how to deal with the creature.

I'm the one who needs help.

Jay turns on the intercom.

"Any closer?" he whispers.

"Nada," Crews says.

"Great."

Before Jay can turn off the mic, Crews asks, "Any updates?"

"Just one: hurry the hell up."

He turns the comm off.

Although he has no evidence, Jay has a gut feeling Crews isn't telling him the whole story, only giving him slivers of the entire picture. It's impossible what Jay has been told is all there is to the future, to the ship, to this creature and the crew. He imagines there's a huge amount of shit he can't possibly know or that could potentially help him, but Crews is leaving all those pieces blank... And Jay's unsure if he's more annoyed that Crews is lying to him or that there's information he doesn't know, information he might've needed for this bullshit beforehand. Going in half-cocked led to many deaths on the force back when. It's irresponsible, stupid...

A teal light appears in the room. Faint, dusty shadows bleed between containers, a dull shine over the metal surfaces.

What's that?

Jay cautiously maneuvers around the shipments until he comes to a place he didn't think he'd return to. Kat's corpse—or what it has become. A flower or something like has grown from the open cavity of her stomach. A stem rises from the flayed belly, bending under the weight of the crimson head at the top. Along each petal are tiny, glistening rows of glowing, teal beads. Fine mist gently sprays from its pale-red center, as though emitting pollen, stopping where its light ends.

Standing before it, Jay realizes he hears faint chiming, a distant bell tower, like before but clearer, nearer... He glances over his shoulder, finding the same sprouting from the bodies plastered to the ceiling. There are three flowers, defying gravity, their heads drooping towards the ceiling and not the ground

If it's happening here, these must be growing from everyone...

His attention's nabbed by the floor around Kat. Crouching, he discovers where the mist reaches, the sludge gradually dissipating revealing a wavering layer of lush greenery... Hyperrealistic, surreal, seemingly fake, as though it's not naturally or organically forming but *created* by technology. Not quite like grass or moss, it seems like it would be plush, soft if he ran his hand over it. Jay isn't that dumb to try. If he wasn't hiding, he'd use his firearm to shoot the crimson flowers...

This isn't good, whatever it is.

Must be the next step for the creature or this shit's evolution.

I need off this fucking ship.

Talons clicking against the floor sends a sliver of ice down Jay's spine. Rushing, he hides behind the nearest container, drawing his weapon and holding it against his chest.

It appears in the blue-green light, stepping out from the nothingness as if an extension of it. Its eyeless, almond-shaped head doesn't move, not breathing, like it's quietly checking on the flower's progress. It leaps over and onto the wall, ricocheting off the metal, and clings to the ceiling. Scurries overhead to the flower patch, doing the same as before. It drops onto its feet on the floor.

Click, click, click. Each talon more distant than the last, until it can no longer be heard.

"What the fuck's happening over there?" Crews says.

"I thought I muted—"

"I can override it, dumbass. It's my system and suit, remember? Anyway, give me an update, now."

"Something's growing on the ship."

"Already know that; why do you think I popped in?"

"What—how do you know that?"

"I ain't blind, Jay. It's growing out and around the damn ship."

"Do you mean outside?"

"Jesus... Yes, yes outside."

"Flowery?"

"Not one I've ever seen but a little bit, yeah."

"Same here, but inside. Counted four so far, but I'm sure there's more."

"Great, wonderful, fantastic..."

"How close are you?"

"About eighteen hours or so."

Jay grits his teeth. "How am I supposed to stay alive for that long after what's happening and that damn dog?" *Dog? I guess it looks like one.*

"Could hide in one of the containers. They're made from space-grade alloy, damn-near indestructible."

Jay looks behind him. One towers over him.

Could I even get in there if I wanted to?

He sees no ladders nor stairs. And if the dog could get in there while he was there, he'd have nowhere to run.

He groans. "Don't think that'll work."

"Well," Crews says, "I don't know what to tell you then. You can hide out in one of the storage closets, or the cap's place, or the airlock and wait until I can get you before it does. Or, you know, you can try to kill it."

Jay reaches for his helmet, wanting to throw it against the wall, but stops. Crews's suggestions are all bullshit, unhelpful. He spits, "Thanks," and shuts the mic off again.

———————

Jay ponders what to do, where to go. He's already covered most of the *Candlewood,* and so far there's nothing anywhere that'd help or protect him. The dog can traverse seemingly everything and on anything. It breaks physics and logic by making noise without air, creating aromas and tastes Jay shouldn't be able to experience. No one should.

What if... What if the gravity was off?

Maybe it needs it to survive; maybe it needs it to maneuver like it does since it breaks physics with gravity on. If Jay could turn it off, maybe the dog wouldn't be able to get to him. It might die without it or be unable to move properly, allowing him a better chance of killing it. Jay doesn't like the plan, still iffy walking with mags on, but it's the only course of action he can come up with. If the dog is dealt with, he could easily hunker down until Crews gets him.

He inspects his weapon, turning it over. The black and white lines weave up its barrel around a slash of white. Twelve green slanted boxes illuminated. *Is this enough to stop it if it attacks me?* Jay hopes as he holds it out, moving around the shipments to the exit. The darkness remains dense in the Main Hall, but once Jay crosses the threshold it lightens, revealing tar lattices climbing up the wall, ceiling, twirling together and forming stalactites. It branches off and curves down the opposite wall, congealing in the ditches flanking the floor.

It shimmers without light, wavering like water yet still static. Pale-pink saplings and buds sprout from the interwoven tendrils. Dozens if not hundreds of them. A wide, giant web runs down the ceiling's center, splitting and whirling around the others, all coalescing before entering the Captain's Quarters.

Jay wants to follow but keeps his morbid, dumb curiosity pushed down. No time to fuck around. Not seeing the dog anywhere, he books it for the Pilot's Room. At the open door, he peeks around the corner.

Nothing.

Treacle covers the console, seeping between keys and splattering the main monitor, and the seats, growing from their backs as though vomited and sealing the upper buttons and switches overhead. It spreads to the bay of cameras, each impossible to see. At the console, scratching away crust from the monitor and keyboard, Jay remembers Crews instructions from what feels like years ago.

```
ACTIVATE MANUAL OVERRIDE: Y/N?
Y.
```

DEACTIVATE INTERNAL GRAVITY: Y/N?

Y.

ENTER.

A vacuum explodes from bow to stern, throwing Jay against the console as his mag boots automatically kick on.

"What did you do?" Crews asks.

"Can you stop doing that?"

"Shut up and just tell me."

"Turned off the gravity. Without it, the dog might not be able to kill me."

"That was a dumb fucking move, Jay. You've only walked in zero g once. Plus, who knows if it'll do anything. It might even *help* it."

"I'm aware," he says, lying. He hadn't considered that, but he was unable to see *how* it would help it. "Just be in position to pick me up before I run out of air."

"How much you have left?"

"About twenty hours."

"Better be in that damn airlock when I'm there then. Cutting it really thin."

"That's the plan."

He mutes the comm despite the little it does.

Moving his feet again in non-gravity is like walking in ankle-deep mud. Entering the Main Hall, he's glad for a moment that he can't sweat, or he'd reek with how much exertion he's using to move.

Hope I didn't fuck myself.

VIII

19:54:49

ABOVE JAY, SEEDLINGS RIPPLE as though underwater. The sludge remains stagnant, though flecks now drift upward, disintegrating before reaching the ceiling. Reminds Jay of the Cap's Quarters. Weapon drawn, it dawns on him that maybe the firearm won't work anymore, that the bullets won't find their target without gravity.

Too late for that now, isn't it?

His boots heave from the honeycombed walkway, stomp down. It's like walking up a flooded stream. His thighs and calves burn by the time he reaches the Mess. *Can't remember it being this bad before... My body must be more exhausted than I know.*

Debris collects on the ceiling in a heap, some congesting the corners, the bathroom entirely blocked off. The stool's still standing, alone on the empty floor. The round table is stuck above, its mags apparently not automatic or broken. Crude patches on the floor are free from smears but aren't free from splashed, dried blood and long, deep scratches. No bodies, though.

For a beat, Jay wishes he knew what happened here.

The next, he doesn't.

Moving past the beds with free-floating curtains, pillows grazing the ceiling and blankets stuck to some of the mattresses by gunk, Jay enters the closet. What trunks were left open are now empty, their contents mounding over the overhead light.

Two trunks at the bottom aren't open, the ones he didn't check before. Crouching, he opens one. Inside, a tinfoil pack of dehydrated coffee, a hydration pack, and an artificially flavored one with banana and peanut butter sticks to the trunk's roof. Jay leaves it unmolested, turns to the other, the inside almost the—

"What's this?"

A laminated, wrinkled polaroid in the back. It's strange and surreal to hold something so old. He can't imagine there're many photographs like this anymore. When he was alive it was all digital; film was extremely expensive.

Must be whoever's family.

The man has short-cropped, brown hair, tan skin, and eyes nearly closed from the big smile beneath. His arm wrapped around a kid that looks almost identical. Behind him is another man; hay-colored hair, green eyes, freckles spotting pale skin. He has one hand on the other man's shoulder, the other on the kid's. Jay flips over the picture. Scribbled in blue pen:

Day at the Park 08/24/58

Alan, Tyler, and Greg.

Damn... The air in Jay's lungs is sucked out of him. He's falling back, or believes he is. He smells rainfall. Eyes wide, fearful, he tries to focus on the here and now, to remain in the closet, remain conscious, terrified the HUSK body is going haywire. But this feeling's familiar, triggered before by the dust. Now it's happening on its own, and he can't stop the taste of smoke cloying his throat, the warmth of the

rented car parked in the airport's parking lot. Rain pummels the windows, cascading down the windshield unheeded by the unmoving wipers. A lit cigarette pokes out from the ashes in the small tray under the temperature dial. Smoke slithers and collects over the couple.

"Do you want to talk about yesterday?" Nicole says.

"Nothing to talk about." He pinches the cigarette and takes a drag, exhales out the open sliver of the driver's side window. His phone vibrates in his pocket.

"Don't be like that, Jason, not with me, please."

"How else am I supposed to be, Nicole? My sister's an idiot and she's going to fucking die because of it."

"It's her life, her choice," she says. "That doesn't make her an idiot."

Another drag, another exhale. He shoves the cigarette into the tray and rolls up the window. "What does it make her then? Not Einstein, I'll tell you that."

"Someone terrified of where they're at, someone who doesn't want a choice forced on her." Her voice breaks.

Jay turns to his wife, noticing the tears falling down her face, dark spots forming on her blue jeans. Reaching over the center console, he takes her hand. "I'm sorry," he says. "For everything... I just don't know how to do this, how I should act or be or what."

Her other hand rubs the back of his. "I know, it's okay. Give her time, she'll come around."

His phone vibrates again. "And if she doesn't?"

Nicole faces her husband, and their gazes meet. "We'll deal with that if the time comes."

Sighing, he leans over and kisses her, wipes her cheek. "So, what do you want to do now?"

"I don't know." This close he can smell the lilac perfume, still faint on her from yesterday. "It feels wrong leaving."

"I know, but there's nothing we can do," he says. "Let's just go home and see what happens."

"That sounds good," she says, rubbing his cheek. "I miss being home already."

"Me too," he says, breaking away and retrieving his cell phone. Two missed calls from work. Not from who he hoped for. He shoves it back into his pocket and pops open the door. "Now, let's hurry and get our luggage from the trunk and get inside before we get soaked."

Nicole smiles, opening her door. "It's a race then."

Cold prickling floods over Jay's face, anticipating tears to pour but not correlating it with the memory. It's sad but the loss opening in his chest like a widening chasm feels as though a piece of him has been taken from his being, his soul. From what he knows, his sister is going to pass, but trepidation forms about his past self, wondering how it plays out, how *he* will react when the cards fall.

Only pieces of the whole story shown, there's more to be revealed. He's fearful now they could come at any moment, the danger of him being thrown into a flashback while being chased by the dog terrifies him. Is it good or bad he's remembering? Is he getting worse or better? *Or has this black shit fucked me up more than I could ever know?* He blinks back invisible tears and returns the photo to the trunk. He can't know, not now at least.

———

Jay avoids the Mech Room. He can't imagine how difficult it would be climbing the ladder without gravity. If he was attacked while trying to manage the rungs, he'd be screwed.

Stopping at the Captain's Quarters, Jay glances up. The giant vine or root running along the center ceiling branches off and vanishes into the gloom beyond. Lack of gravity must've removed some of its outer layer revealing beaded ridges within unfurling indentations. A pattern of some sort, unfolding to only reveal more of itself, stretches all the way back toward the bow.

Double-checking his weapon still has full ammo, even though he hasn't shot it yet, he enters the room.

The tar wall's gone, leaving no flaky piles or drifting motes. The overhead root runs from the door into a newly formed opening where the tiny holes once were. Jay stays to the side, looking into it from an angle. Headlights on. The well—doesn't know why he attributes it to a well—has a weathered, puckered rim, ascending to narrowing heights with an end he can't make out. Its walls are blackened with streaks of gray, slick and grooved, gleaming in the light.

No, wait...

They're breathing, like disturbed water, a slow whirlpool and pale waves emerge from internal depths to break the surface, returning below once more.

Maybe I should turn off the mags and see where it goes?

Crawl through the bowels of this thing...

What am I talking about? For what? To see what? It's not worth it.

He turns away to find the cot gone, no sign of the pillows or blankets. Glances to where the imploded corpse was, and it's still there, glued to the wall and corner. Jay peers into the well again, shakes his head. A MLID's under a tiny splotch of ichor where the bed was.

Scraping the gunk away, he retrieves it. He removes the one from before and slides in the new one. Jay holds his breath and listens intently...

Nothing, thank God.

The APC opened, he checks the audio's off and plays the chip. It's a V-MLID again, and the captain appears on screen.

Behind him is a bare, empty wall; no background to pinpoint his location.

His blond hair's disheveled, greasy to his shoulders. Wide, charcoal veins web up his neck and over his chin, climbing his face and uncurling beneath his hooded, sickly, yellow eyes. He hacks into his dirty sleeve, leaving darkened blood, then says, "I don't know how long it's been. A day, a week, a month? Don't think it matters now. The *Candlewood* never made it to its destination. Couldn't even move a hundred clicks from my earlier entry. We—it—are immobile."

Coughs into his arm again, coming away with more remnants of oily red. "What was the point of this? Of that shipment? What the hell am I doing?" He shakes his head, grimacing. Gasoline wells in his tear ducts and slides down his face. Eyes dim to honey yellow. He grits his teeth, some crudely filed down into rounded points, others left the same. All are gray. "I wish they would stop for a minute. Anything for peace and quiet. They're. So. Damn. Loud." Veins bulge in his temples. "On and on and on about sowing. Whispering and screaming. Overlapping. Constant, even when I manage to sleep. Why are they bothering me? Can't they see I'm sick? And that *fucking bell*."

Ashy snot dribbles from his nose. He futilely tries to inhale it and faces the camera, his eyes now bright yellow with blue specks. "I've ordered a self-quarantine since showing signs after opening that damn container. Obviously, what was inside there wasn't meant for us, or was exactly for us... I don't know. It shouldn't have been opened, shouldn't have been touched. And because of this, of *me*, we can't land. To top it all off, we're seemingly in a dead zone. No long-wave comms, only short, which doesn't do us any damn good. The E-Pods have been powered on, just in case."

He chuckles. "Not even Cathy has a damn idea what's going on with the ship, me, any of it." The blue chips in his eyes vanish and the yellow dulls. "Quiet, please!" He grabs his head, screaming, "Can't you just... Just give me a moment to myself!"

His fingers pop at the joints, elongate, grow. Nails widen, extend into curved, sharpened ends. The flesh of his hands is scattered with gray veins and sinew. "Sow what? What the hell do you mean? Confine? Propagate? How—why—*what?*" The captain begins to sob, clasping his hands behind his head. "Just let me be, please," he whimpers. "Can't you just leave? Can't you stop ringing that damn—"

The video ends, and Jay's body goes cold. A minute passes, two, and Jay moves to close—The video returns, and Jay's hand freezes on the monitor. The man's yellow, distant stare encompasses the entire screen. Pricks of aqua are visible at the end of an immeasurable tunnel. Tendons or muscles raise around them.

"I understand," he says. "I. Get. It."

The captain backs away from the camera, revealing a mangled amalgamation of his body and the creature stalking the *Candlewood*. Torn sleeves vomiting bulbous, black bones contort in odd, ugly angles. A skeletal, crisscrossing shell geysers from his bleeding lips, his teeth growing and twirling, creating a pattern of gray bone, doubling-back to force his head into an almond shape. His sternum spirals with taut flesh, a grinder turning muscle and bone and innards into configurations not meant to be made.

Before Jay can make out his bottom half, the video ends.

———————

The afterimage of that hideous abomination hooks deep in his mind despite closing the screen. His arm drops, dangles at his side.

What the hell happened here?

Though he knows, an idea and map of the events bubble up into his consciousness. Someone had the disease or whatever it is in the shipment. The captain caught it when he put in his hand. It ran rampant inside him, turning him into the dog, and afterwards, or during the transformation, the captain murdered the crew members. For what purpose, Jay hasn't a clue.

He looks at the well again.

I don't know what any of this means. The crimson flowers, the pink saplings, the dog, the bell... He might've been a detective when he was alive, but this is way beyond him, beyond human interference.

"Gotta get off this ship," he mutters.

Mic on.

"How close are you?"

"Uh... not much closer than before. Seventeen hours or so, if nothing else happens."

Mic off.

Jay leaves the room with his weapon at the ready.

18:38:09

Only an hour has passed, but swatches of vivid green have appeared across the ceiling, undulating yet unmoving, like within the edges of its being possess a life of its own. Pink buds are replaced by shimmering chartreuse leaves of honeydew opening to a fuchsia stigma and bronze filaments. The fuchsia is ever fading, endlessly melting away from the center yet never emptying, never dying.

Whatever's happening, it's happening fast.

Maybe I don't need Crews. If the pods are on...

Jay remembers they're in the belly of the ship. They must be huge since Crews told him they couldn't fit anywhere else. Fear rising, his hands and feet clammy and prickling. Afraid what's growing will affect him even more, and the more time spent here is more time that the dog can kill him, or he can be absorbed by the growth or turn out like the captain or anyone from the crew... Jay follows his gut. Crews doesn't need to know. There's more to him, things Jay's ignorant or oblivious of. Even Kat warned Jay before her passing, but he pushes aside his skepticism. Jay'll figure out Crews once he's safely off the *Candlewood.*

He can keep his money.

Not knowing how they work or where they'll take him, Jay doesn't care. Like all the problems that popped up once he arrived on the ship, he'll deal with them as they come. Although it sounds careless, it's better than being trapped.

The Mech Room is like the others. What wasn't put away or underneath something is heaped against the high, sloping ceiling. The floor, tool bench, even the railing overlooking the engine is coated in sludge. Jay darts for the ladder and pulls his feet from the floor. With an imagined clunk, then another, his boots stick to the rungs. One cautious, heavy step after another, he descends.

Making it to the catwalk, it's like entering a starless space. It was dark before, it's now absolute, oppressive, as though grown here. Even with the headlights on he can hardly see more than a foot or two ahead. The interior wall is a hole, absorbing what light is cast over it. He makes it to the second ladder at the opposite end of the catwalk.

At the bottom, he sees a dim, blue light in the distance, a teal dot millions of miles away. As he nears it, it grows, becoming clearer; a flower appears. It's like the others before it: black peduncle, crimson flower, pale-red center, and petals beaded with glowing blue-green. Sprouting from the imploded remains of who Jay believes is the mechanic. Mist-pollen sprays from the flower's center, creating an enclosure of something like grass rippling on the floor. The air's awash in light blue.

What the hell are these things? What's their purpose? Should I kill it or leave it be?

Above the corpse, Jay finds a raised indent descending the wall like a bolt of lightning, disappearing behind the body.

His temples pound with frustration. There's so much he doesn't know and it's impossible for him to find out, to understand. He doesn't think even Crews knows what the fuck is going on. Turning away, he decides to leave the flower be and search for the E-Pods.

Enormous.

Vast.

Overwhelming.

Soon, the engine towers overhead, an oblong, oval-shaped, copper mountain bolted to steel straps and bending contraptions lost to the darkness above. It reminds him of the *Candlewood* itself, a battery for a titan. Intricate wires and tubing roves over its rusted frame, sliding flush and out into the ship's hull. A hodge-podge of crude work clearly only for use, not looks.

It's even reached here too.

Pitch blossoms over its bottom, growing like roots up the sides. Jay focuses ahead and continues on. When the engine slopes upward, it gives enough berth for the E-Pods near the bow. Six cylindrical, tall, gunmetal casings lie diagonally in a dock aimed toward narrow walls. Between them is a narrow, square protrusion Jay assumes is the generator. It's tan-colored with two buttons on its side and a gauge on top.

All the pods are open. Each have low ceilings, blue cushions lining the back, and a monitor panel built into the side.

Jay glances over his shoulder into the absolute nothing, waiting for a sound... Sweet silence. He moves to the nearest pod and leans inside, tapping on the screen. It remains blank. He pushes out of the pod and inspects the generator. One button reads ON, the other OFF. Gauge blank like the screen. Shrugging, he presses ON. The gauge illuminates, and white text winks into existence on the black-blue screen.

25% POWER REMAINING

Lights flicker in only one pod, casting jaundiced light onto the floor. Jay hurries inside, entering backwards, his head resting against the cushion. He puts the weapon to his waist.

I'm finally out of here. I can live again. Do something else. Be someone else. Won't repeat the same mistakes or be so much of a dick.

His smile grows as his excitement builds, hope filling his thoughts.

Loading finishes on the screen, and data appears. The pod raises a little beneath his feet as the door slides closed. A video stream appears on the screen's upper-right corner. It's outside, the emptiness of the engine room. More information is calculated—weight, height, analytical data of how long the voyage will take to its predetermined destination, and even more things he doesn't understand nor care about. Jay just wants to get the fuck out of there.

Launch Y/N?

Y

Adrenaline pumps through him as relief washes over him. He wishes he could cry, wishes he could release all the pent-up frustration and joy in one form or another, but even that, he feels, was taken from him. He watches the outer hull slide open, revealing space. No stars nor planets; no lights anywhere.

The pod undocks and suddenly drops, then it's like floating on water. He hasn't realized his fingernails are digging into his palms.

Waits.

Waits...

Waits...

Air, stillness, palpable, wrapping around his limbs—

Something crashes onto the pod's roof. He screams, crouching, looking up. Nails or swords scratch across metal, high-pitched and grating; something wet slaps the side of the pod. *That fucking dog!* The monitor showing outside dies.

"Launch!" he shouts at the machine. "Launch now! Confirm launch!"

He pounds on the screen, the sealed door. Send them both into the void, cast the dog into space and let it float forever. The floor drops slowly, a little, like before. Jay hears, or imagines he hears, steel grinding against steel.

That gunk must've gotten into the railing.

He hears more damp slapping against the hull, more scratching and tearing and gnawing on the roof, the door, the sides. A cacophony of reverberating, clattering, and crashing noise hammers into Jay's ears. He grits his teeth, wishing he could cover his ears, eyes, wishing he could just leave the damn ship, be somewhere safe, home, wherever or whatever that may be. Jay wants to return to the cold storage and be in the aether, the in-between, again. The future's not worth it. This isn't worth it.

It roars, a shrill noise unlike anything he's ever heard, a thousand nails on a chalkboard. The monitor explodes with brilliant light, and he winces, throwing up his arm. His body becomes weightless as the pod leaves its station. For a second, he's cheering, for a second he's airborne; then he's falling face first, helmet smacking the door, a splinter running up the bottom corner. The vehicle's trajectory changes, leaning forward, left, right. After he pushes off the door, he's thrown against the side.

The door jerks open when the pod hits the floor, and Jay rolls out without mags on, forgetting they were off in the first place. He drifts toward the open hatch.

Boots ON!

They come to life and stick to the curved, interior hull, violently thrusting him into a standing position on the wall. Vertigo and nausea wash over him, and he closes his eyes, grimacing from the whiplash of everything hitting him at once. If Jay had a real stomach, with actual food and bile, he would be puking into his helmet.

At least that's one positive thing about being not human.

Opening his eyes, he finds the pod toppled over on the ground. Jagged scars run down its side and roof; white streaks through some of the ichor. Bottom frayed, with broken treacle and seeping tendrils spreading limply onto the floor. The open hull where the pod would have left through wasn't starless space but sludge... *Moving. Teeming. Growing.* Not only has it covered the bow but the stern too. Jay guesses it cocoons almost the entire ship now.

No way out.

His mind leaps from the fear of being trapped to the dog, almost forgetting being prey. Drawing his weapon, he aims down and ahead. It's nowhere to be found. It takes a moment for him to understand how to move on the wall, to take a slow step forward, which is actually down, then another. From the wall to another wall—no, from the wall to the *floor*.

This is awful.

Unmagging one foot and lifting his knee up to his waist, he takes one uneasy, awkward step and places his foot flat onto the ground. He does it again, nearly losing his balance before his other boot reaches its destination. Once he's steady and the world's righted, his sense of balance returns, and the vertigo dwindles. He rechecks his surroundings. Still no damn dog...

But I can't leave now.
No way of escape with or without Crews.
I'm going to be stuck here.
I'm going to die, again.
Asphyxiate. Drown without water.

Space, the *Candlewood*, everything closes in upon Jay, encroaching upon his mind. His lungs flutter, trying to catch his breath. Futility barrels over him. Death. The end. A prisoner in a cell within an even bigger cell.

I have to get out.
I have to leave.
I have to do something, anything!
But I also want to quit, give up.
End it all before it becomes too late for me to be able to.
Rather a bullet to the head than be without air. I had the right idea the first time.
Maybe lay down for a bit beforehand, sleep for a couple hours before the finish line.
How long has it been since I've done that?
A month? A year?
How the fuck does time work here—

It dawns on Jay that the dog isn't attacking him, even after standing still all this time.

It attacked the pod, hellbent on stopping it. Now he's out in the open, emotionally and mentally exhausted, but it's nowhere. No clicking talons, no slapping filth.

Frustration grows.

What the fuck does this thing want?

Does it want to kill me or not?

Maybe I've been wrong and it doesn't want to?

Maybe it didn't want to be in the Pilot's Bay either?

Maybe it wants me alive?

To stay on this awful ship?

"For what?" he screams. "What the hell do you want!"

Silence.

15:47:09

"Are you close?" he says, standing where the pod fell over, aimlessly staring into the dusk.

"Closer, yeah, but not *close*. Why?"

"Can you see the ship?"

"Yup."

"No, like, can you *actually see the damn ship?*"

"Can't fucking miss it."

"What's it look like, then?"

"Why does that matter?"

"Just tell me what it looks like."

"Like a huge shit with two ends on the top and bottom. An opening in both, I think, can't tell this far out. A bunch of growing vines or something dispersing out on top, some are together, creating a shape. Looks kinda like flower petals a bit, but black as fuck. Without the weird glint it has, I wouldn't be able to see it."

"What—"

"Oh! And some other things are poking out around the middle, but can't really make them out."

"What about the bottom?"

"About the same at the top, no petals, though. Just kinda a large vine or tube with an opening at the end. Not dangling or anything."

"Can you still see the airlock entrance?"

"What?"

"Can you *see* or *not see* the goddamn airlock entrance, Crews?" he spits through clenched teeth.

"Well, yeah. Sorta."

"What do you mean 'sorta?'"

"All right, calm the fuck down, Jay. I know vaguely where it is, but with all this shit I can't *really* see it."

"So, you *shouldn't* have a problem getting me out?"

"As long as it doesn't thicken or something, yeah, should have no problem."

"Why?"

"Why what?"

"Why would it matter if it's thicker?"

"Would make it harder to get through, obviously. I don't have those kinda tools with this ship to get through it, and you don't got anything on your end either."

"Can't you shoot it out or something?" Jay looks up, as though Crews's ship's above the *Candlewood*. "Doesn't the ship have anything like that?"

Laughs. "Renter, bottom of the barrel. No fancy gadgets or anything worth paying extra for. Its sole purpose is to get from point A to point B, remember?"

"Wonderful."

He switches off the mic.

15:30:57

Without any plan to follow, Jay slumps against the nearest wall.

On his ass, he spreads out his legs, the mag-heels keeping him grounded.

Shouldn't have taken the job.

Shouldn't have killed myself, either.

Shouldn't have done a lot of things, but here we are.

He raises his hands toward his face but stops, clenching them into fists. "God this helmet is fucking annoying."

But it's more than the helmet; it's everything. He wishes he could take off the suit, wishes he could relax and take a nap, wishes he was capable of eating because he misses the sweetness of fruits, the saltiness of fried food, the sugary carbonation of soda. A want more than a craving, a hollow yearning that can only be filled by the one thing he can't do.

What I wouldn't do for a burger, fries, and a large cola right about now...

What did I eat before I ended it?

Probably something cheap and quick, gas station hotdogs or cheap fast food.

Jay lets his hands fall. He feels heavy. It's not his suit that feels heavy, it's like his limbs are filled with cement. Muscles and joints replaced by stone. His mind threadbare, always too tense, too tight, always preparing to run or escape only to be thrown back into the enigmatic mix of this hellhole.

Jay groans.

"Stop it," he tells himself. "Focus on things you know and can actually change."

The ship's being enveloped by the sludge.

The dog is—was—the captain, or what's left of him.

The crew is the red flowers with the blue pollen.

The shit inside the ship is changing, evolving. Probably happening externally too.

He can't escape, possibly because the dog wants to keep him

on the ship for unknown purposes. It may not let him die, either, but he doesn't want to test that theory.

The pods don't work.

"I'm fucked."

He feels like crying but can't. However, dry sobs come, wracking his chest.

Why do I care if I die now, when I didn't before? I have far less than I did then. I had a family, a wife, a job, a place to call home. All I have here is this fucking suit and gun and the stupid dog that can't make up its mind with what it wants to do with me. No family, no wife, no home. Not even this body is mine.

Do I really want to keep living with so much uncertainty, with so much lacking in fulfillment, gratification?

He takes a minute then: *Kind of, yeah. I don't want to waste this second chance, although it's a shitty one. The future might be better than the past. Might have a better go here, too, once I'm off this thing. And who knows, Nicole might be HUSK'd, or I might be able to get her HUSK'd. Ashleigh too. I could have my family back, my wife, and I'm sure there's more work to be had now than there was back when. More planets and possibilities with space travel... So, I guess I do want to live.*

He wants to get off the ship.

Wants to do whatever he can to ensure that happens.

Slowly, he pushes off the wall to his feet and sighs. Draws his firearm and makes his way back to the ladder.

14:59:41

Moving around the ladder, he continues to the bow, where the crimson flower's teal mist reaches; greenery flows outwards, undulating. Jay raises his weapon, makes it as point-blank as he can, and pulls the trigger. No kickback or no recoil of the shot, unlike the last firearm. Feeling only a weak vibration up his wrist, a green bullet zips from the barrel. The flower explodes into glowing maroon ribbons, teal goo splashing the wall. The stem wilts in the non-air, squirting more blue-green fluid. It putters out, and the pollen dissipates. The green dwindles.

Headlights on, he inspects it closer. It's no longer moving without moving but pulsing slowly, like a dying heart. Green fades to gray, then black. The raised, root-like thing behind the corpse shrivels, its taut flesh pulled tightly over clusters of tiny ribs. Reminds Jay of a snake skeleton.

A guttural shriek explodes in the distance, reverberating off steel, echoing down to Jay. His chest rattles like a bass drum. *If it's pissed off, I must be doing something right.*

It'll be coming for him. *Great.* He rushes back to the ladder, kicking off the mags, and climbs frantically.

14:08:59

The root's wilted in the Mech Room, and Jay finds the same in the Main Hall too. The beaded pattern is pronounced against the brittle, dehydrated skin. Seedlings, mud brown and dry, are breaking away, turning to ash like burnt leaves. What green there is is graying, no longer encroaching into more areas.

Another cry lances through the silence from the ship's front. Jay runs the opposite direction. The dog can't be found in the gloom, even with his headlights, but he feels its presence. He can't pinpoint its location or where the guttural shrieks originate from though.

Through the Cargo door, he passes through the narrow spaces between shipments and gets to Kat. She's the same as the person he found in the Engine Room. Without thought, Jay raises the weapon, aims, and fires. The red flower explodes, splashing the back wall with illuminated teal, and the stalk shrivels. Green-blue pumps out from it, quickly stopping. The root climbing up the wall dies the same as the other. More clusters of beads rise.

The explosion of pain barreling through the *Candlewood* is deeper, crunchier, brimming from depths where stone's ground to dust.

It's really pissed now.

He moves back through the containers, the mag boots too heavy to shuffle as fast as he likes, knowing the dog ought to be coming for him soon. Breath heavy, yet he's not sweating.

Still not used to that.

He side-steps out into the clearing by the exit hull door and the WASTE container. Above, he sees the collection of human flowerbeds, blue mist spraying onto the ceiling. Verdure spills from a pool on the ceiling, each beat pushing it farther and farther out. There's so much pollen he can hardly make out the bodies, but Jay can see the colorless roots expanding from the people. They're thicker here, providing more power or life to whatever's growing on the ship.

"Okay, get out of your damn head," he says.

Raises the gun. Fires.

One flower winks out of existence.

A roar erupts from somewhere behind him.

Fires, again.

The second bursts into teal ooze, splashing the ceiling and floor, defying no gravity. Both flowers wrinkle, curl inwards, and the blue glow fades to nothing.

Another scream, louder, *nearer*. A deep, guttural, hoarse war horn. A bellowing titan. Agony of the gods. His hands are trembling, and his teeth are clenched. He furrows his brow, aims, fires.

Misses.

Fuck!

Tries again.

Misses again.

Fuck, fuck, fuck!

His arms are shaking, horror rolling up from his false gut. He can't aim, can't shoot. Limited time and bullets. His shoulder moans from being held out and up for this long.

Don't screw up. Just aim and shoot. It's not even moving!

He pulls the trigger and misses once more.

Jay wants to scream and rip off the suit; wants to lay down and cry; wants to kill the damn thing. He shakes the nerves from his arms, hands, takes a deep breath in, and aims again.

Steady; be steady.

Gently lays onto the trig—

Thrown from his feet, Jay crashes and skids across the floor. He smacks the wall, the back of his head temporarily ablaze with fiery pain. Something hisses but quickly stops. The crack in his visor bolts into his sight line. A dull throbbing comes from every nerve. It takes a second to realize what happened—and another to realize he no longer has his weapon.

He looks—

The dog's on top of him, four boney talons digging into his thighs and chest. Jay rams his fingers into its oily torso, holding its almond head back, struggling to move away because it's impossibly heavy for its size—a blur of black and holographic sheen and gray. The cracks in his visor splinter even more, like lightning in a storm, white static blocking his view. The headlights turn on, casting a shadow over its head, shadows pooling and filling the craters pocketing its face.

The dog's head peels apart like a shell in four directions, gummy bonds snapping like gum, filth spilling over him. A steaming hot substance, like gravy or pudding, spreads over his suit. He prays it doesn't burn through, prays the dog's nails don't puncture it. A multitude of pink tendrils swim out from the inner lining of its head, toothless workings of what must be its mouth. Teal light winks to life at the bottom of its elongated gullet. Pollen swirls and mists from it, illuminating crevices and gouges that make Jay want to revolt, to not hold it any longer, his flesh recoiling from bone.

He attempts to jerk its head to the side, but it's like moving a statue; so strong, dense, so damn solid. Tries again and it gives a little, the tendrils slithering from its mouth whipping away, searching for something to grasp. Another forceful wrench and two feet slide off him, and the other legs follow. The weight of its body working against it. It's enough for him to roll the opposite direction, onto his stomach. He forces himself to his feet—mags on—and finds the firearm drifting inches in the air, six green lights still glowing.

He snatches it as it turns to him, its internal veins or roots or vines growing, fanning the non-air. Jay spins around, raising the firearm, and blindly shoots. The bullets rip through the dog's muscular side, passing through entirely and charring the wall behind it.

No screaming.

No pain.

But it halts for a moment, and Jay takes the chance to fire another. It's split through the right flank, opening another wound. Its leg collapses, toppling over. The crooked legs tremble, attempting to limp forward on only three. Pulls the trigger again, again, again. The dog's legs give way as gore bursts from the bullet holes in its belly. Still the dog tries to reach Jay without arms or feet.

Jay fires once more, but nothing comes out. The green lights along the side are red. He tosses the weapon as he stumbles back against a container. Breathing labored, the world foggy and fuzzy with cracks, the inside of his suit is sweltering, or he imagines it to be. Jay frantically searches for another weapon close by. Finds nothing.

Bones pop and groan as they whine and bend. Sounds like they're breaking only to be put back together. The dog's abdomen bubbles and swells until it bursts, vomiting steaming tar into the non-air. Treacle cools into a glossy wax. Tendrils or peduncles retract into the inner lining of its flayed mouth. The green-blue light steadily dissipates, pollen vanishing.

Jay doesn't forget the last time the dog went down, although this time is much different. He heaves his legs forward to it.

When the black stalk slithers out from its mouth and the buds beginning to peel back, he grabs it with both hands. Feels like hot putty covered in syrup, even through his gloves. He pulls and stretches it across the floor.

Mag off.

He raises his foot and stomps onto it.

Mag on.

The boot locks to the floor. Jay tightens his grip and wrenches it upward. It rips in two, black and teal liquid spurting and splattering him. The end under his foot jerks and rattles wildly without a head, spitting ichor until it stops, wilts. The part he holds dies rapidly, turning into what looks like jerky.

Tossing it away, he stands over the captain, the dog. He waits, watches. Hands at the ready. But after a while, nothing grows or shoots from the body; the wounds don't heal; ligaments don't move; gaping holes don't open or close. Nothing more hideous than its corpse is revealed. Silence weighs like the world's on his shoulders, but it's welcome.

"Fucking *finally*," he sighs.

He turns, clearing his cracked visor with his arm, not adding much visibility. Too exhausted to care about the gunk on his suit, he leaves it. A deepthroated, grating roar floods through the ship like a sonic boom. Containers rattle and skid across the floor. His limbs fly back, Jay's fake innards bounce off his ribcage, and his helmet's light extinguishes as the O2 in his suit stops. Stale, stagnate air sits within his helmet, but he inhales smoke, burnt coffee flooding his taste buds. The boot mags

turns to the doorway leading into the hall as his wife comes in, wearing her navy blue blazer and slacks, a belt, and shoes; blonde hair done up in a bun. "She call back?"

Jay scratches his neck, the stubble coming in. "No." He sets down his cell phone, picks up his mug and takes a sip. Already cold. He watches Nicole go to the carafe and grab her thermos from the cabinet. She fills it and screws the cap on as she looks at him. "How long have you been up? I didn't feel you come to bed last night."

"The better question is: When was the last time I slept?"

"Jay," she says, frowning. "You can't keep doing this. She said no."

"Yeah but—" His phone vibrates and he quickly checks it. Work. Puts the phone back down.

"They're going to fire you if you keep dodging their calls, you know?"

"Let them," he mutters.

"Don't be like this, Jason." She comes to the table, setting her thermos down, and lays her hand onto his shoulder. "You can't keep waiting for something that may never come."

"She's my sister, Nik. I can't just... Can't just go on as she dies."

"You're not." Sliding over a chair and sitting, she leans towards him. She rubs his knee. "We went down there, we asked her to come, we tried our best. But she still said, 'no.' There's

nothing else we can do. We can't force her to come or get treatment."

He sighs, rubs his face. "You're right. I know you're right, but my mind... It can't just stop thinking about her, what will happen. She's the last family I have, you know."

She nods. "You still have me, dear."

"And I'm grateful." He takes her hands. "I don't know what I'd do without you."

"Probably still be sitting at the kitchen table checking your phone."

He laughs. "Yeah, probably."

She kisses his cheek, and stands, grabbing her drink. "But I gotta go. It's Monday, so it'll be extra busy today. Might be late coming home too."

"All right," he says. "Call me on your lunch?"

"Will do. Love you."

"Love you too."

Everything's brought back to life, and fresh air fills his lungs. Until now, the memories seemed to be brimming with melancholy, but that one was nice. Not sad or depressive or somber. A warm, comforting slice of life moment between husband and wife he wishes he could live in forever.

Too bad there is so much shit going on to enjoy it.

It clicks in his head after a beat.

The dog's dead.

But there still was screaming.

The dog isn't making the noise.

The ship is.

"... What the fuck is going on, Jay?" Crews shouts. "The ship shook—it *fucking* shook!"

"Sounds about right," he says. "Whatever it was killed the power for a couple seconds. Even took out my suit's power too."

"You need to figure this shit out before it kills you or ruins your suit. If your air's gone, you're fucking dead. And another..."

His voice trails into the background as Jay notices his O2 counter. Before, it was around fifteen hours, but now... He has about five hours.

Nowhere near enough to last until the bastard gets here.

The hissing.

The dog tackling him.

"Fuck," he moans.

"What?"

Silence.

"Jay, answer me dammit."

"It's the ship, Crews, or whatever's on the outside." His eyes widen, searching the air for answers not there. "Thought I could stop it, kill the plants, the captain... But I'm out of ammo and it didn't even stop it. Only pissed it off." Looks to the last dangling flower on the ceiling, the blue pollen feeding the moss above. *There's probably more I don't know about.* "Now I don't have enough air."

"How much do you have?"

Silence, again.

"4:57:46."

"Well... shit."

IX

04:55:39

I'M GOING TO DIE *here for sure now.*

In a frenzy, he searches for the key, moving pitch from the floor with his boots, raking with his fingers, scrambling between containers despite his inability to fully see.

Going to drown.

Layer after layer gives way like ash, smearing his suit, kicking up motes that surprisingly don't trigger a flashback.

Don't think like that. One of these might have air.

He moves from one side of the room to the other. Soot spirals around him, drifting above. Particle clouds float overhead.

Where is the key?

Where is the fucking key!

He gives up the search mid-way. Wasting time and energy he doesn't have. It must've been kicked around at some point or stolen by the dog—who the hell knows? Instead, Jay hustles to the Medical Bay. He ignores the transition happening around him; he can't view most of it anyway.

The Medical Bay's the same as he left it except for the two misting, crimson flowers—one in the corner, another from the western wall—and vegetation encompasses the entire floor.

121

The bead-patterned root roves over the ceiling, down the wall, and to the corner. Chartreuse leaves of honeydew with fuchsia stigmas and bronze filament poke out from it, swaying.

He avoids everything the best he can as he searches, turning over what's still on the floor, sifting through the ceiling corners congested with medical tools and equipment.

Nothing. Nothing. Nothing.

How the hell is there no extra air in a medical area?

What kind of fucking shit-show was Crews running?

His loathing for Crews grows, and so does his suspicion of a larger story he doesn't know. He leaves and makes for the nearest Storage Locker. Maybe he missed something the first time. The shelves are ramshackled from switching from no gravity to gravity then back again. He swipes away rows of hydration packs and dehydrated food. Some float around him, others cling to the wall and ceiling. Row upon row thrown aside, it gives way to nothing worthwhile.

Jay wishes he could drink some of them.

Eat some of them.

Sleep.

Anything normal, anything that removes him from what the hell's going on and tether himself to the world he once knew.

He just wants this all to end.

Him or the job, he isn't certain.

But he's wasting time thinking, wishing. Jay rushes to the cafeteria.

A flower hangs out through the open bathroom doorway, pollen showering the walls and floor. Greenery spreads over every surface like spilled water, coming toward where he is. He hadn't realized there was a body in there.

Doesn't matter. Ignore it. Focus.

Jay kicks away empty packets and containers, shoves the

overhead, upturned table and stools around, searches through odds and ends of an oblivious crew that didn't know what would befall them.

No suits.

No O2.

No help.

In the Bunks, he rips off mattresses and tears pillows and scrapes away what pitch there is with his fingers. *There's not a damn thing here!*

In the closet, opening each closed trunk, he empties them madly. Things drift and roll and stick to the wall and ceiling—tablets and gadgets, clothes and jewelry, empty snack bar packets, digital photographs framed in metallic silver and in cellophane, memories no one will ever see or care about.

There has to be a spare, an emergency canister. Something, anything. He's astounded there's not a single one to be found. Perplexed people wouldn't carry an extra in a place that doesn't have any at all. They should have a ton just in case. He's dumbfounded that if the ship was breached and air was lost, they would be left to die because of their stupidity.

Dropping everything, he makes for the Pilot's Room.

Buttons and chairs and switches and windshields and the bay of monitors are plastered in sludge, outside and in. Monitors are useless; chairs abandoned, obsidian edifices. He removes some sludge from the keys to turn the gravity back on, because with the dog dead, what's the fucking point?

Weight wafts over him. He imagines bones popping, settling, and the echoes of objects crashing to the floor. Waits a few seconds and turns off the mag boots.

Should've turned it back on before searching the ship.

Just another thing I should've done.

Small lines illuminate the windshield, rippling emerald encasing it. Light rolls over the glass like the tide, as though standing before a waning sea or a valley brimming with lush grass in a calm breeze. Transfixed, Jay's wild eyes gloss over; a waxing, waning sound whispers in his head. No longer a bell, warping into an alarm—no, *a siren*. He catches hints of exhaust, gasoline, and burnt rubber. Bitterness and bile coat his mouth. Nausea makes him salivate. The strobing peridot becomes red and blue, and his breath leaves him when

he should've picked up his phone , shouldn't have ignored the calls from his work, from the station. He might've been able to stop it, despite the impossibility. It had nothing to do with him. No amount of preparation could've halted the events that occurred.

Dumbfounded, he stands at the police tape, the strobing lights of the police cruisers painting the terrible scene red and blue. A firetruck in the rear matches the pulsing rhythm. His leadened hands hang to his sides, one still gripping his phone as though it's the only thing anchoring him to the pavement. The surrounding crowd is deaf in his ears, a numb cacophony miles away.

"Sir? Sir, are you okay?" an officer asks him up close. "Do you know one of the drivers involved?"

He nods, or believes he nods, and says, "Yes." The blue sedan wrapped around the tree, facing him, it's hers. That's her car. See her? In the driver's side, behind the splattered blood plastering the shattered windshield? Bits of flesh and hair and matter tangled among the wreckage? Yeah, that's her. That's my beautiful wife.

"Who do you know? Which one?"

He wants to point it out, like that'll somehow distinguish it from the red car on the other side of the road, parked sideways, snaking burn marks on the street trailing its rear wheels. The driver sitting on the curb, head in hands, vomit between legs, surrounded by police.

"The dead one," he blurts. "The one not alive.*"*

Ghost tears break like a dam and stream down his face. He can even feel the wet, taste the salt reaching his lips. His insides feel hollowed out despite not being full to begin with.

Takes a deep, rattling breath and

Exhales as the coroner lifts the white sheet from what remains of Nicole. Although her face's smashed in, she's still the most gorgeous woman he's ever seen. Clean of gore and glass, what pale-blue flesh and blonde hair there is tells him she's gone, as though somehow before this there was some miniscule chance he was mistaken, wrong, the driver in her car not her but someone else. He prayed for it, but not all prayers are answered.

The coroner says, "Is this your wife?"

Cell phone still in his hand, the plastic digs deeply into his palm. It vibrates or not, he's not sure of anything anymore. Unglues his tongue from the roof of his dry mouth, opens his lips. "Yes," he says after a moment. "That's her."

Jay's mind feels like being wrung out, twisting and tightening in an attempt to release all the memory fluids it has soaked up. Guilt and fault swirl through him, filling his empty head, despair drowning him with prickling cold. Logically it isn't his fault, but without a doubt he feels it's so. There are two parts of him conflicting, the real him and the HUSK, each fueled by uncertainty.

"Jay?" Crews chirps.

He replies but only mumbles.

"I have an idea," he continues.

"What?"

"Destroy it."

The idea pulls him from his maelstrom of depressive thoughts, pulls him from the storm raging inside and wanting nothing more to pull him into the undertow.

"Destroy what?"

"The thing covering the ship."

He groans.

"How can I do that?"

"I don't know, but I bet there's something explosive in the Mech. Use that to kill it. Didn't you say there's a hole or whatever in the cap's place?"

"What if there's nothing there?"

"Then it was nice working with you."

Turning the mic off, Jay mutters, "Wish I could say the same."

04:18:59

It sounds suicidal. Stupid. A waste of time.

What other option is there? Might as well try to kill what's apparently trying to kill me, distract myself from feeling like an absolute failure.

But what if the memories come while I'm doing this?

If I do or I don't, it doesn't really matter now.

God only knows what comes after all this. Could get a lot fucking worse.

The glistening, chartreuse flowers along the raised roots covering the Main Hall ceiling now have stigmas of glistening yellow, no longer light fuchsia, and lime green filament. Thin, purple veins—*vines*—spread out from under the never-ending melting flowers and weave around the beaded patterns surrounding them. The lines appear and disappear down the walls, rooting into the flanking ditches, moving under the honeycomb floor.

It reeks of wisteria and magnolia, of roses and dianthus. Pungent, overpowering vanilla, a tinge of sweetness. The aroma cloys at his throat, like he has potpourri lodged in his esophagus. He laps mouthfuls of air in a failed attempt to get the floral taste out... Somehow, he's able to taste and smell without air, like the dust is seeping through what must be micro-openings he can't possibly see in his suit.

What the fuck is going on...

He doesn't understand any of it, how it's happening, why it's happening, how and why it's so beautiful and welcoming and warm. He imagines it should be hideous and ugly, a monstrosity with protruding eyeballs and tentacles, innards spilling from unimaginable beings with thousands of orifices. Not this. Not an eye-watering, beautiful nursery.

Is destroying it even the right decision?

He stops before entering, the doorway outlined by a trellis of blue bellflowers.

Is it?

The dog did try to keep him on the ship, didn't try to murder him until he killed things himself. It was protecting the flowers, guarding what it's becoming. For, or from, or why, is incomprehensible, the reason unknown.

And what's covering the ship... *That scream.* It feels pain on some level, though it hasn't retaliated. All it has done is continue to grow, harboring, incubating nature, transforming the ship to some type of greenhouse. It's always been passive, idle.

Should I try to kill it? He leans toward a baby blue flower and sniffs the sweetness emanating through his visor. *Am I the intruder or the infection? Or is it? What would happen if it managed to reach more people? And what if what I'm thinking is completely wrong and by doing nothing it will kill innocent people? Can't take that chance.*

He enters the Mech Room to find the beauty hasn't reached there yet. Tools and objects are scattered on the tool bench, the floor, and by the metal balusters overlooking the engine. If he would look over the railing, he guesses he'd discover more brick-a-brack below.

04:02:31

Jay discovers a snub nose firearm under the tool bench. Gun-metal, hefty, its barrel outlined in ebony with a strip running down the side and curved grip. Along the other side are five rectangles, only two lit orange.

I'll take that.

Putting it to his waist, he continues searching. Catty-corner with the entrance and tool bench is a crevice clogged by debris. Underneath, there's a knee-high container.

Pulling it out removes some of the pitch on the floor. He sets it flat carefully and struggles but finally pops open one latch then the other.

Gray Styrofoam—*can't believe they still use this shit*—encases a metallic square with copper prongs along its edges. It reminds him of a computer processor, a chip. He gingerly lifts it from the casing. Surprisingly light, with a slightly bowed back and a handful of differently shaped ports along the edges and center.

Double-checking the case, he sees a square sticker plastered to the opposite side. It's a jungled pattern of numbers, letters, and other symbols. Beneath the pattern, in small letters: scan with APC for user manual and instructions.

Jay opens the screen. The ship's three-dimensional gridwork appears. Along the top of the screen are options he apparently missed from being too focused on the investigation and not being killed by the dog. He pokes the SCAN option and the screen fills with a real-time image of the wall he's facing. When he points the APC to the pattern, a gray outline of it appears then changes into a text document. White lettering on black.

He mumbles to himself as he looks through.

THE iARN-XBW3790K™ — THE MOST EFFICIENT PROCESS-ING CHIP OF 2192.

Isn't it 2700-something? Jesus...

In microscopic text beneath: WARNING: FLAMMABLE AND EXPLOSIVE.

The internals are copper tubing, four barometers full of mercury, and micro-linings containing liquid silicon. The iARN-XBW3790K is used as a catalyst for non-syncing wiring and connections, able to create a stable route from two entirely different systems. It can also be used for wireless connections. Most commonly used on ships programmed with outdated automatic or AI functions.

Seems to be like an emergency, heavy-duty band-aid.

It was very expensive, at least in 2100. Probably why there's only one; or it was left and forgotten for six hundred years. Either way, Jay takes it.

I should be able to throw this up into the well then shoot it. Might be too old to explode, but it's all I got. If it's a dud, then I'm back where I was twenty minutes ago.

03:40:18

In the short span he was gone, the Main Hall's verdure had grown exponentially or brightened to a level it's difficult to stare at directly. Jay isn't positive which; both may have happened. Every area, every crevice in the vaulted ceiling, every ditch along the walkway, seemingly every single atom making up the damn ship breathes with breezes of glowing, sparkling emerald. Flowers radiate their own shades—pink, yellow, blue, violet—emanating from brilliant stigmas and filaments. The beaded designs once hidden now sprout like honey-gold seedlings, lime green vines spiraling around them.

It's all-encompassing. It's eye-burning. It's a nostril-clogging and throat-congesting vortex of magnificent, awe-inspiring familiar, alien life. Jay's sight smears like melting wax, like oil paints running together. His brain can't process all the

strangers, all the damn people. Where did they all come from? He thought his phone always vibrated before, but now... Endless phone calls and dozens of unprompted visits and invitations blur past day by day. Always with apologies, with prayers and hope and him being in their thoughts. Dissociating, on autopilot, he detaches from his body and emotions. He's numb to the core, watching himself move through life, not being truly present. Too far gone to cry; even tears don't seem enough to do justice to what happened.

He can't handle scheduling the funeral; his brain too fried to accomplish simple tasks. Nicole's parents did it all, sending out invitations and directions and everything else. At the viewing, he stands silently, shaking hands, thanking the stream of people in black for their condolences. His eyes are bleary, stinging. Body exhausted. Sleep a distant memory despite the ample time off his captain ordered. Focus fixed ahead, he refuses to move in the direction of where the body that was once his wife lays in the ivory casket. Hours drudge by until they are instructed by the director to their cars to follow him to the church.

So removed from the situation, Jay doesn't realize as he leaves the funeral home that it's the last time he's going to be in Nicole's presence.

His phone buzzes when he gets into the car, but he doesn't check it.

He's reeling from the Main Hall and its decadent hues or the memories or both. The flowers along the ceiling have reached the walls, and buds dot the spooling vines, hanging above his head. There's too much going on, too much color and sound even in the silence, and his eyes are glued to the moving but unmoving foliage growing from every direction and surface. Keeping his head down, the walkway still barren, he sprints to the Captain's Quarters.

03:20:39

Surprisingly, the room is the same as before. It has yet to flourish. The corpse he used to trigger a memory doesn't even have a crimson flower. Mags on, he stands beneath the well. The narrowing walls are still slick, undulating, *breathing*, streaked with gray waves that appear and vanish under the surface. Its end and top are unseeable. A deep-seated yearning opens in Jay, a longing to lift, to climb into it. He smothers this malformed idea; it's ludicrous. He focuses on what he must do.

The processing chip in one hand, the snub nose in the other. Mags off. He crouches a little and springs up to the well as he chucks the chip into it. Its vacuum takes it, seemingly stronger the higher it goes, but soon it sticks to the right side, embedded into the muck.

Keeping himself beneath the well, headlights on, he stretches his arm inside and takes aim. The chip gleams against his light. Nothing else does.

Two bullets. Make them count.

The first goes wild, a flash of orange quickly consumed by the well.

He breathes in... Holds it... Pulls the trigger...

It hits its mark.

A fiery plumage explodes, erupting down the well, throwing

Jay to the floor. The gun leaves his hand on impact. Viscera and sinew spill and splash the other side of the well, falling freely from above. Purple-green flames—*how the hell?*—spread over the walls. An impossible, ear-splitting, distorted scream sounds, and Jay futilely attempts to cover his ears.

His insides feel like they are going to explode, as though his false innards are inflating with fluid, pushing against his sternum and ribcage; his eyes expand in their sockets, pressing against his temporal lobe or whatever organ rests between his ears. Another roar follows and everything's thrown into absolute blackness save the tapering flames above. Suit and ship offline, the vacuum unheeded, Jay's immediately wrenched from the ground and slammed against the ceiling. What little air he has in his lungs is forced out of him. His heart frantically beats, and his throat constricts as he tries to take in the tiny amount of O2 left in his helmet.

Hanging over the well's edge, he can't help but look into it before a second explosion of fantastical-colored plumes he didn't expect. Like being suddenly hit offline, everything turns back on and Jay slams onto the ground, the cracks in his visor spreading to the upper rim. A shrill, guttural wail reverberates in his ears. Static covers the visor save for two sections near the eyes that hold it intact. His mag boots turn on. Oxygen floods his helmet, and he hacks as his lungs inflate.

Rolling over, he strains his vision to find the gouge in the well—a void, star-speckled space on the outside. Its skin flaps in the vacuum like wet, tattered clothes. Fire climbs higher and higher, but soon peters out, dwindling, dissipating...

Shit.

"What the fuck was that? An explosion?" Crews blurts.

"Which one?"

"*Which one?* Does it fucking matter?"

"Guess not," Jay says. "Yeah, it was. Tried my best."

"Did it work?"

"You tell me."

"Doesn't look like it... Whatever the hell the thing is, it's grown. Taller, thicker, like a tree trunk but rubbery, slippery looking. That bottom part, too, but it's split into even smaller, longer, ribbony parts, like roots or some shit."

The O2 counter reads *02:48:21*. Even if he was capable of the impossible, to stand, run to the pilot's room, and steer the *Candlewood* toward Crews, there simply isn't enough time. Hell, even if he were to jump out of the damn ship he wouldn't have enough air to make it.

And it feels so good to be lying down for once, to not be hunted.

His joints and muscles sigh, adjusting to the hard floor.

Nothing to be done. No one can reach me. There's no saving me.

It's over. Done. Did my best but still came out in the red.

Thin, dark filament crawls over the well's wound. It crisscrosses over the hole, overlapping, patching his first and last attempt to kill, it until it's no longer there.

He imagines tears again, imagines them running down the sides of his face, imagines his eyes stinging. Cold prickles his face and nose. Takes a long, rattling breath...

No point staying alive to only asphyxiate. Rather die fast than deal with drowning in space.

This second life is fucking bullshit.

He goes to speak but doesn't.

What's the use of telling Crews? What's the point of any of this? May as well give into the memories popping in and out, stop fighting against them to focus on this stupid hellhole. Rather know who I was than what I'll soon become.

Crews has been talking, apparently, and Jay cuts him off.

"Don't worry about it. I'll figure it out."

He cuts the intercom.

02:40:31

He feels a comfortable familiarity, like coming home after eons away. Tranquility blows over Jay. He inhales the bitter aroma, tastes the tobacco, smells smoke and coffee, and the well gives way to

him sitting at the kitchen table, an open pack of cigarettes laid out next to his cell phone and a half-empty cup of cold coffee in his hand. Jay's not sure what day it is. It's night outside, he can tell from the window above the sink, but is it the same night as the funeral or has it been days since and he's survived off only smokes and coffee?

Their—his—house groans against the wind, settles. Silence weighs over him, over the entire building. He takes a drag and exhales, new smoke joining the gray smog overhead. Takes a sip, grimacing, too tired to get a refill. His cell phone vibrates for the hundredth time. Resistance unfurls inside him, hesitation, fear. He grits his teeth. The last time he answered the phone... He doesn't want to think about it anymore, just wants to get through the thick of it, because if anything else happens—so help him God—he won't be able to function anymore.

Where do I go from here? What happens next? The luster of being a detective gone, the allure of tomorrow and the future dissipated. With his wife on the other side and his sister at the door, what's the fucking point?

He releases the mug, grabs his phone.

Ashleigh...

Really, she's the last of his family now... Maybe she'll re-consider his offer now he's alone? Maybe the guilt will drive her to not be such an idiot? With Nicole's life insurance soon to be paid out, he could afford her to fly down, even afford her treatments—not all, but some. Whatever the amount, he'll pay to keep her going. Nicole would've liked that, would've wanted that.

Always a saint, even when she's not here. A far better person than him, always.

Ignoring the dozens of voicemails, he dials Ashleigh's number.

"Hello," *a man's deep voice answers.* "This is the Thosassa Police Department. How can I help you?"

Jay's thrown back into his mind, his body, the ship.

A moment later: *Why would the police answer?* The unwanted answer instantly springs into his mind. *Suicide.* But he can't know for sure, can't know how Ashleigh's life turned out. The memory leaves more questions than answers. Jay's still adamant on knowing how things played out, wanting nothing more but to ignore the reality of his present situation...

What is *the point, really? Nicole. Ashleigh. Both long gone by now, and even if they're HUSK'd, would they remember me? After this many years? Or are their minds wiped like mine before getting infected? If Crews hadn't told me I had a wife and sister in the restaurant, would I remember? Doubt it. I wouldn't have been any wiser...*

"Should've said no from the get-go," he mutters. "Gone rouge the moment I could, did something fucking enjoyable instead of working."

Standing, staring into the well, he balls his hands. Frustrated by what's to come, by the job, from wasting his second chance at life and failing that too. If given another opportunity, Jay's uncertain it would be any different. He is who he is, and history repeats itself more often than not. He's cast into the unknown, desperate to find his way, to make sense of it. He doesn't know anything else, so why wouldn't he?

But here he matters little in the scheme of things. What happened to the *Candlewood* crew was before being HUSK'd, and this disease—or whatever it is—was going to happen with him here or not. The captain might've wanted him to remain on the ship, but the reason remains beyond Jay. Maybe it was for what's happening now, maybe not. Maybe it was just a fucking disgusting, hybrid malformation of a man and alien working by instinct alone or innate instructions given by something outside the ship. Maybe—

Enough. This is the end. What's done is done.

No bullets left, no other way of going about it. He lets the well's whispering curiosity of the past snake forefront. He turns the mags off. He jumps, helping the vacuum's pull.

The rim and ceiling pass by. The slick, undulating walls do too. Gray cartlidge rise to the inky surface, protruding only enough to make out millions of teeming beads matching the design of the beads on the roots. Green lines weave around each. Then it's gone, below. The wound he inflicted has fully healed; he can barely tell it was ever there.

Farther up, the gray appears again. Honey-gold washes out the green, and the beads begin vibrating. Warm, obscure light radiates through the thin, sleek wall. It pulsates with his heart-beat, the beads inflating with his lungs. Each breath of wind wafts over him from above in sync with the surrounding golden light, brightening, rolling down the well to the bottom he can no longer see.

Deeper, higher, Jay's passed through its bowels.

Narrowing, they tighten around him as they inflate. Before he realizes, he's stuck, pinched by the walls engorged with golden light and a porous fluid molding to his form. It fills and expands into all his crevices. Blotching his visor and vision until nothing can be seen except the golden light in the dusk.

His visor cracks more, one hole now shattered. The other, his last, cracks, widens, on the precipice of exploding over his face. The air counter becomes a flurry of incoherent numerical and algebraic symbols; only two numbers he can understand remain. Jay's chest tightens the more the well attempts to digest him. Shadows fringe his eyesight. Consciousness ripples with the ever-growing tension, the ever-breathing lights, the ever-expanding fluid. He feels the APC shatter, the wrist-strap disintegrating.

"Just fucking do it already," he spits between clenched teeth.

It must listen, for with an abrupt, immense squeeze, Jay plummets into unconsciousness.

X

Δ1:φ9:∞x

A S HE STANDS IN *the cellar of the coroner's office beneath the Thosassa Police Station, a wave of déjà vu washes over him. The draftiness of the place without a draft, the sterile lights, the cold radiating from the cement, it's all familiar. He feels the same emptiness in his chest, the gnarled knot in his gut, the prickly clamminess of his palms, one gripping his phone for dear life. Feels like he's dreaming; everything has a layer of surrealism, fakeness, as though any minute someone will tell him this is all a big misunderstanding.*

The white curtain on the opposite side of the window is pulled open. A woman with tied-back auburn hair and brown eyes behind glasses, standing by the sheet covering a person, says, "Are you ready?"

Mouth dry, words lost, he nods.

The sheet's pulled away, revealing Ashleigh, his sister, his beautiful, blue-gray sister. Her hair is slicked back, eyes closed, and her lips are no longer pink. There's a bruise around her pale neck. "Is this her?" the coroner asks.

He wants to shake his head, wants to punch through the glass, wants to jump atop the metal table and dig his fingers into her chest and force her heart to beat once more... But he nods again.

A hand on his shoulder. Jay looks and has totally forgotten that Officer Tuttle accompanied him here, didn't realize there was someone else in the hall. "Want to talk upstairs?"

The coroner covers his sister, and Jay quietly croaks, "Sure."

Jay awakens on the floor of the Cap's Quarters.

First I've been unconscious since being brought back; first dream, too, if it counts. Felt like all the memories before it. Now that I'm thinking about it, I haven't been tired enough to sleep in nearly two days. The HUSK must adjust based on what's going on...

Looking up, straight ahead, the well above no longer has slick walls or breathing gray bones or buds or golden filament. It now erupts with iridescent flowers endlessly blooming outward, phantasmagoric purple-black petals speckled with breathing stars. Lustrous, yellow vinery intertwines around cosmic stems then becomes lost within the dense foliage. Jay's mouth waters. His eyes sting. His gut bubbles and his groin hardens.

Stop looking.

Stop looking.

Stop...

It feels like he's drowning, going blind; his erection painfully hard and his gut burning, spitting bile. He can't stop, can't remove his eyes from the dots, the beautiful, delicious nature.

Stop!

He jerks his head and faces the wall, and the bodily reactions cease, deflate.

After a few moments to adjust to normalcy, he pushes himself up to a sitting position. His O2 timer is busted, but he guesses he has a little over an hour left, God willing. Avoiding the well, he wonders what happened, why it rejected him.

Did I not taste good?

Too many artificial flavorings?

It refused to give him the satisfaction of a quick death, one that satisfies his curiosity, and now Jay must deal with a grueling, miserable way of doing it on his own. He would rather anything besides asphyxiation.

Bringing his legs inward, placing his feet flat onto the floor, he rises. Immediately feels lighter than before and realizes the mags aren't on, but he's not being pulled up. Also...

No more sludge; nothing dark.

It's all coated in the greenery from the other sections of the ship. Rich, wonderfully wavering fuzzy green is everywhere, all around him. It's scaling the walls, the ceiling, giving way to the well. Without another option, Jay carefully walks to the exit.

"Still alive?" Crews chirps, his voice staticky.

"Unfortu—Yeah, still here."

"Where the fuck have you been? I've been trying to reach you for over an hour. The ship looks fucking insane: branches or some type of wooden spider webs have grown from the top part, poofy green shit coming out of those things. What they're made of, I have fucking no idea. And the bottom, Mother..."

Jay becomes enamored. It was beautiful before, but now... It's a dense jungle, amazing, fantastical. The chartreuse flowers overhead are the size of his leg. Flower-heads droop heavily from above, their once bronze filament yellow-white, spooling onto the floor and hanging in the air. Their stigmas engorged, tiny buds beading the top, smoky pearl swirling within. They poke through the honeycombed walkway, blossoming in real-time as though reality is sped up.

Maroon veins pump light into wide, brown trunks curving

up the wall from the ditches. The aroma is unimaginable, marvelous. Wisteria, magnolia, dianthus, jasmine, lilies, oak, pine, redwood, mahogany, soil, dirt, compost—a haphazard hurricane of floral, nature, and loam scents. Dozens of fleeting flavors waft into his gaping mouth—vanilla, mint, clover, horehound, citrus—so many others he can't possibly name before they vanish from his tongue.

Everything ripples, everything's alive and moving without moving, and God is it astonishing. The colors seem like he could scoop them out, as though they're pools within shapes of flowers, trees, vines. So enrapturing he has the urge to taste them, to consume them, to roll in their impossible beauty in the hopes of drowning and being reborn nearly as beautiful as they.

He doesn't know where to look, for even the ground is mostly covered in plantlife. The ship's stern is sealed off by it; all the front rooms choked with layers of unfurling vinery and girthy roots and splintering tendrils with prickly, pink bulbs.

The raised, black indent that once ran down the center of the hall retches petals and branches and leaves and ferns, and it's so *fucking* exquisite Jay reaches out to touch it, to confirm if it feels as warm and soft and welcoming as it appears. But he stutter-steps, tripping on something, and looks down to discover a subtle footpath snaking through the forest. Maybe not so much a path as a small, bare patch he can use to navigate.

Crews's voice in his ears is millions of miles away, a tinny din over an awe-inspiring storm.

Wonder what the Engine Room looks like, the Med Bay. The Storage Lockers...

The lower the floor slopes, the more flurry of iridescent life brims. Bursting and corkscrewing from every crevice and opening there may be, even ones he never knew.

The Cargo Bay's door hangs on the bottom hinge, rust crawling up it from the bottom corner. Top's crumpled, as though a giant hand crushed it. Umber fibers ascend the opposite side; moss and leaves sprout from the space between it and the wall. The window's empty; not a glint of glass remains.

Jay enters.

The containers are like the door, abandoned and rust laden, ancient. They are monolithic remainders of a bygone age he feels like he was never meant to be a part of. Copper dust fills their locks. Decaying leaves sprout from dark roots entangling them. The crimson flower remains, unchanged, spraying its teal mist where Kat died. Her bones are gone, giving way to a trunk rising and cascading over the ceiling, the birthplace of more grass-but-not-grass seamlessly blending into the forest hanging above.

Doesn't really matter now, does it?

Jay gives into curiosity and slides his palm into it.

It's not mist, nor fog, nor spray.

In the hollow of his glove, tiny seeds or grain gathers. Thousands. Millions.

Focusing, now knowing what they are, he watches closely as they hit the ground, defying gravity like the flowers on the ceiling had. The seeds don't disintegrate or vanish but are carried away by the emerald waves. Jay drops them then stands beneath the cluster of people above.

Trunks billow out of the center, converging into a massive one covering the surrounding area. The flowers Jay destroyed a lifetime ago are gone except the one he couldn't kill. It's still sprinkling its seeds.

He goes to the WASTE container. Open now, weeds and ferns and other green things plume from it, slipping onto the floor.

The breathing green and moss, the trees above and where Kat is, everything in each room, absolutely everything surrounding him on this Godforsaken ship connects to an enormous, rigid pod resting atop the box.

The captain said something about this when he put his hand in.

Jay maneuvers around nature to get near it. He reaches and gently touches it. Four lines appear down each segment then they peel apart and bloom in unison. An inner design of miasmic, white-speckled pitch curls infinitely inwards. A tidepool. A draining puddle. A melting mirror. Silver tinged, reflective. Empty and absolute. Stars wink into existence beyond, beneath, to be replaced by kaleidoscopic planets and distant, rolling celestial bodies, for those again to be churned and reveal deep, wet jungles; towering, featureless, gray trees; vast plains of head-high, orange weeds; cerulean valleys surrounding a tremendous hollow, mimicking the fuchsia-tinged sky. Over and over more images are given and taken, more peeks into other places, other worlds, flashing by until it stops and only a reflection of Jay's battered helmet and shattered visor meets him.

Revulsion rolls through him, but he *can't* look away, like when he gazed into the well. A somber desire rises from his chest, filling an utter loneliness he didn't know was there. Crawling up his tightening esophagus, prickly cold tension breaks and like rain, trickles down his body, collecting in the emptiness of his artificial gut, running off to his feet. Jay doesn't understand this feeling, why he desires something he doesn't know nor comprehend, why it feels like this silver pool is a long-lost lover who has finally returned to him.

The visor in the reflection crumbles like broken glass while his in reality has not. Rounded, dimly-glowing, white-blue crosshairs overlay his bleary, brown eyes. Pale cheeks, average-sized nose and lips. The same face he saw at the park, hardly worse from wear, which makes Jay's revulsion heighten. He knows the image isn't real, but he should still look worn out, beat down, bruised and sore and pale with hollow, sunken skin and protruding bone, his physical being illustrating the nightmare that's been wrought upon him in this hellish place. He's been through an unimaginable nightmare, yet it only appears as if he stayed up a little too late fucking around on a computer.

This isn't me.

This'll never be me, no matter what HUSK or shell I may be in.

What shows isn't what's true.

The stranger in the pool presses the side, releasing latches connecting the helmet to the suit. It hisses and lifts up.

What's above the brown eyebrows isn't a scalp, forehead, or hair but a void, rivulets of mercury pouring down his face. The man in the reflection turns, and the space is concave, encompassing the entirety of the back of his head. Within lies an amorphous, globulous mass of silver. Bending his arm back, he watches him shove his arm into the mass, the liquid streaming down his neck. He pulls it out unsoaked, not a drip of silver, as though the fluid isn't there. Removing his hand from view, the face of another person—another man—is shown.

Jay.

The *real* Jay.

He sees closed eyes, dirty-blond hair, and light, thin eyebrows. The ears are small, a dainty nose, average-sized lips, and a pronounced chin. The eyes open—bottomless, crystal blue sclera fractured with gray. His mouth opens, and between the toothless maw another pool surges up the throat. Black instead of silver, glistening without illumination. Two sets of five pale fingers pierce the surface. One covered in blood, wearing a gold band—

Jay screams, and *real* tears flood his vision. He wrenches from the pool, the flower, the box. Stumbling, tripping on a root, he crashes onto his ass. Doubling over, sobbing into the hands that can't reach his face, tears collecting on the visor. Releasing the pain. Releasing the past. Exorcizing everything that was taken from him when his second chance was forced upon him. He can't remember everything, but enough has broken through for him to cry and scream until he is empty, completely, utterly barren of the pain and sadness that lead him to his suicide.

"What's going on? Jay!" Crews in his ears. "Jay!" Crews is so fucking loud he's impossible to ignore.

"Get me off this ship!" he roars, spittle flying, on his knees, gripping the helmet tightly. "Get me off this fucking ship or so help me God I'll fucking drive this thing into the sun! I can't—I can't do this anymore."

The comm cuts, crackles. A broken, red message plays along the bottom of the visor: EMfRG𝔜ΣY OV⊕RI≈E. E¬Ø∂GY C∃SERVⱢTIⴖN DE∀∠OY∃D.

"What do you want?" he shouts at the plants, trees, vines, shouts at everything and anything surrounding him. "What do you want me to fucking do?"

What's my purpose here?

Did I ever have one?

This would've happened with or without me.

I'm useless.

Nothing.

An imposter among beauty.

Jay collapses into the fetal position, wrapping his arms around his legs.

I want to be home.

I want my body.
I want to be normal, human.
I want to be anywhere but here, alive or dead.
I want my life back.
If not, just end it.
End me, this ship, every damn thing.
Can't—
His fingers scramble to the helmet latches.
—do this anymore. Can't—
The right lifts, pops out; air hisses.
—wait. Anything's better than this, anything.
The left follows.
No fucking use.

He's muttering, tear-laden, blubbering, yet unaware of what his physical form is doing. Detached from the body and mind, from all that's artificial. "So sorry." Talking to someone. "I'm so sorry." To himself, the *Candlewood*. "I didn't mean to—" To the plants and the flowers. "—fail everyone." To his past self, to the real Jason. "Ashleigh. Nicole. Crews."

His sorrow and sympathy extends to everyone and everything he's ever come into contact with, from people of the past and present day to those affected by his failures in the future.

He removes his helmet.

Vision once filled with white noise now has clarity.

The foliage even grander, more striking, more enticing.

Rich and astounding, it's almost impossible to believe something like this exists in the world.

If I touch them, the colors will wipe away like paint.

They gently sway like an invisible tide whispering through them.

But he can't hold on anymore, doesn't want to...

Jay takes a deep breath...

??:??:??

And breathes out...

Inhales, exhales...

I'm alive.

I'm fucking alive.

"The plants must be creating enough air for me to live..." *or has there always been air and I never knew?*

Briefly, a smile grows over his face then turns into a grimace, his brow furrowing. Jay tosses aside his helmet, stands, and wipes the tears with the backs of his hand. Still stuck on the *Candlewood*, the only out he had taken from him, again. Sorrow gives way to anger.

This damn plant.

The exit is barricaded by congested vinery and other fibrous strands of nature he doesn't know. The lever to open and close the Cargo Bay door is corroded in place. Even if Crews got there, he couldn't get to Jay. He can't imagine what the rest of the ship's interior looks like.

Jay glances at the full leaves growing from knobby, milky beads protruding from them; the stalks heavy with distended, six-petaled flowers that seem at any moment like they could pull apart, birthing their wonderful hues.

Even though it's beautiful, I still hate it. If it won't let me end this miserable place then it should rot.

Turning to the WASTE container, unheeded by his visor, audience to the greenery.

I was wrong before. The well isn't the brain or heart, that must be some other important part. It's this seed-thing. The rest of the BS throughout the ship is the innards. Maybe it's growing something above the well; or maybe not on the ship at all, but somewhere else entirely in a way humanity couldn't possibly comprehend.

Jay grabs a thick root and tugs it, finding it's firmly burrowed into the metal hull. It doesn't give any more with two hands than it did with one.

If only I still had the gun.

If only I wasn't here.

Jay peers into the mirror pool again. His face remains the same. Not his *real* face, but the HUSK's. The reflection bubbles, forming into another shape, but the horrors are fresh in his mind, and he quickly turns away.

He looks at his hands, the box... Before he can hesitate, he plunges his arms, up to his elbows, into the mercury. He keeps his head up, away from the silver splashing and spilling over the rim, trickling between the roots, splattering Jay's suit. The fluid's like lukewarm mud.

He can't feel a bottom past his elbows. Standing on his tiptoes, reaching deeper, nearly to his shoulders, he feels nothing, his fingers frantic in swamp water.

Guttural wails boom all around him, sending tremors through the jungle. Jay clenches his teeth, standing as high as he can on his toes. Screams rise to blistering heights, ear grating, head rattling, lung emptying. His fake insides shake like the vines overheard. The ship's power goes out and his mag boots die. Lifting from the floor, he scrambles for purchase with his hands, groping at the seemingly bottomless, porous liquid for anything to hold onto. He feels a rigid rope to the far right, and stretching as far as his arm would go, he snatches it.

Each resounding roar is a hammer to Jay's temples, a battering ram to the gut. Blood or non-blood coats his mouth, and something wet pours from his nose.

"Doesn't feel too good, does it, fucker?" he says, his legs above his head. "Now you know how I feel."

He pulls himself until he's up to his neck in the fluid. It's cold on his flesh despite the heat radiating through his suit. It sticks to his face like glue. Tiny, fiery pins prick his skin with each drop. Jay doesn't care, can't care. Wants to die anyway, so pain is par for the course when there's nothing to lose. But he refuses to die before he kills the damn thing.

Another rope's felt to the far left, and he takes it in his free hand. He drags himself deeper, to his lips. His gloved fingers coldly burn.

The plant's screams become a cacophony of titanic sound, the shifting and rending of muscle and bone of a god, the Earth wailing with every earthquake. He follows the rope, moving his hand farther down. It comes to a sloping, sinewy surface. Moves his left hand where his right is. He bites his bottom lip and pulls as hard as he can.

Jay stops, breathing heavy.

Tries again and again, and finally it gives. Syrupy treacle floods the mercury. Before he's lifted to the ceiling, he grips the left rope with both hands and repeats the process. The silver pool bubbles and fades to a decadent scarlet, frothing with holographic foam. The roots deflate and shrivel in his grasp.

The gorgeous life surrounding him dwindles, waning into dull drab, like someone turned down their glow. Decay and pestilence scurries through the ship. Petals quickly crumble into wet mush. Vines shrink and wither; buds dehydrate into dust. The wavering green now powers a dying being, and Jay guesses it's spitting rot back into its system.

Jay smiles, belly laughs—

The roots finally snap, but he doesn't give a shit. With his arms free, he tosses aside the umbilical cords. As he reaches the ceiling, he watches the jungle die.

Tears come but he keeps laughing, keeps smiling.

With each scream, his consciousness winks out—a blink of nothingness then a glimpse of all the decay. Mercury and crimson globules float like bubbles around him, expanding when they reach surfaces, covering the rotting plants in sleek red. The pool empties revealing another bottomless well coated in inky liquid, gray cartilage poking out. Tattered, tarnished gold viscera drapes from its walls.

Then, the ship has power.

Gravity switches on.

Jay collides with the floor among the blood downpour.

XI

*S*ODIUM LIGHTS BLUR PAST. *The road is empty. Headlights cut the night. Silhouettes of forestry atop towering cliff faces.*

Jay isn't certain where he's going, but he has to go somewhere, do something, be anywhere but his house, anywhere that reminds him of them. He'll know where to stop when it comes.

His cell phone rattles on the passenger seat. Whoever's calling isn't important to him. No one's left who matters. Wife, sister, parents. All gone. What's the fucking point of picking up the phone?

What's the point of waking up and going to work? For what? Money? What value does that have for him when what he worked for is no longer in the picture? Something he pursued like everyone else in the world is suddenly worth as much as the gravel kicked across the highway by his tires.

And for who? Who would he work for? Who would he wake up to, come home to, spend time with outside of work and on the weekends and during the holidays? Himself? Right now, he wants to put as much distance as he can from himself, from his mind. Sever the two at the fucking core and hope it quiets the maelstrom of pain wreaking havoc through his head, chest, gut. How can he survive tomorrow, the next? He can't fathom the coming years without them.

Hills give way to flat, harvested farmland. Moon and stars hidden behind clouds he can't make out. Streetlights dwindle until the only light is his own.

The gas needle hovers near E, and he doesn't want to stop unless it's his last. He ignores a Quick-N-Go. Doesn't want to deal with the exhaustive task of paying for gas, exchanging words with anyone. Then the needle reaches E at the moment the Luditz Motel's blindingly bright sign pierces the night. Color TV. Pay-Per-View. Adult Movies. The works.

It's as good as any place, he thinks, turning onto the cracked tarmac. He parks in front of Room 8.

Jay comes to an unknown length of time later. The surrounding world brims with purple-gray rot; hillocks rise from the floor, run down the walls, pile in the corners. The door leading outside entirely hidden by decay, containers buoying in low tide. His helmet is lost beneath the fetid goop. Like melting lard, it drips in globules, viscous pools oozing over the ground. The vital organ once above the container is nothing but an ugly thing of porous gunk. As Jay sits up, he realizes two facts: there's a chance of escape with the jungle gone; and if the plants were generating enough air for him to live, he had killed his only source of O2. He doesn't have time to search for his helmet, though.

Really fucked myself, didn't I?

Maybe I'm wrong and there's still air aplenty?

He gets onto his feet, staggering, and grabs a nearby container for support. A mishmash of brown, gray, and mold green absorbs his hand. Lurching from one muddy box to another using waist-high lunges, he makes it to the empty doorway.

Trenches of umber rise over the floor, slippery and sucking underfoot. The beautiful, hypnotizing ceiling is a masterpiece aflame, globs and fatty strands of colors and decomposition collapsing, dripping, streaming endlessly in thick rivulets. The stern's impossible to see—Jay can't really see much of anything but the mishmash of sloughing plantlife.

He slips and falls to his knee. Stands, steps then slips again but catches himself on a vine with an overcoating that seeps between his fingers like butter. Flicking it away, he wipes his palm across his chest and moves as fast as the putrefying nature will allow.

Filth rolls over passing rooms, revealing even more sewage.

His lungs flutter, hitch. Working double-time to keep up with the thinning air.

I was right—I did fuck myself.

The curtain of vinery and nubs of flower dotting the airlock entry has become a flat waterfall of mud. Jay closes his eyes, pinches his nose, and takes a deep breath before barreling through it.

He clears his face before falling onto the slippery floor. Crawling, pushing up, his toes find purchase and he rights himself, lurching down the corridor. Not much plant matter made it to the airlock, though some slowly oozes toward the ripped barrier.

Never did figure out what happened here.

He trudges into the white room, boots squishing with remnants of decomposition.

Jay reaches the exit and slaps the START button despite the room not being able to cycle air and seal.

Something grinds behind him. He turns to find where he

believes the barrier has been torn. A transparent wall slides up and connects to the line along the ceiling.

Oh... Guess it wasn't ripped.

A white tile on the wall lifts revealing a touchscreen. Green-texted data runs diagnostics and code; numerical figures and text scurry past his deadening gaze. Completing, it shows the air levels are below 25% and dropping steadily.

Jay's going to drown when he's so close to leaving.

Pressing buttons on the monitor, he manages to find Crews's intercom listed under NEARBY WIRELESS COMMUNICATION. After randomly tapping more things, it puts him through.

"Where are you?" he bleats, leaning against the wall. Filth and sweat cover his face.

"Jay? How the—what the—you know what, fuck it, I don't care. Fifteen minutes, tops."

"Don't have that," he forces out. His tongue feels furry, enormous; his wide eyes bulge against the rim of the sockets. Temples beat like drums. Clammy toes and fingers prickle, and his body's five times heavier, bone or whatever his skeleton is made from groaning.

"Story of our life. Can you drift?"

"No." He shakes his head. "No helmet."

"*What!*"

"Just—just get here."

"Doing my best."

"Do better or you'll be getting a corpse."

He slaps the monitor and the comm window closes.

Jay turns to the narrow lockers along the opposite wall, but he's too exhausted to move, to search through them. He shimmies to the exit, puts his back to it, and drops onto his ass.

He closes his eyes and props his head back.

Calm down. Being worked up uses more air.

I have every right to be worked up.

Why am I, anyway?

Didn't I want this? To die?

That was before I had a chance to live.

Or maybe I never did in the first place; maybe I was so fucking wrapped up in the hellscape I was lying to myself. A good thing masked by bad.

I do that to myself a lot now, lie.

And now I have a chance, a real second chance, to restart. To not deal with loss, pain. To possibly find Nicole and Ashleigh and bring them back.

Will they even remember me?

Just shut the fuck up and focus on staying alive.

He wants to open his eyes to look at the air meter, yet at the same time, he doesn't want to know the numbers. Dull yellows and greens web his eyelids, beating with his rapid heart, his hyperventilating.

So close. So damn close.

He peels his eyes open in spite of himself. He's lying on the floor but can't remember doing so. His ear's to the ground, cheek against the cold metal. He's facing the exit. He blinks and the world blurs like the melting stuff within the ship. Doesn't want to blink again, afraid of what he may see, but he can't fight it and gives in. Blurry; reality awash in pinkish gauze. Something is doing something miles away, resonating over the horizon. Grinding talons violently hook into steel flesh; boulders and earth are devoured by endless layers of ribbed teeth; some shit crushed by other, bigger shit.

He's so fucking tired. He can barely feel his face, let alone his arms and legs, but the floor moves under him. Drifting into—sliding across the air or non-air or who the fuck cares?

Bright red explodes over his lifeless, glassy stare.

Blood pumps from severed arteries.

The screen is an abstract illustration, punching through the warping reality with a yellow: 8%. Alarms sound. Bells ring. Choirs sing. Heaven and Hell clash and clatter, and angels weep and devil's roar. The world is coming to an end while alloy crashes and rattles. Gods are shouting sounds like the shrieking well—

Thought it was dead.

Guess I couldn't even do that.

—a symphony of jarring noise tornadoes into his ear and drains out the other, soaking the underside of his face. He can't help but smile, can't help the euphoria flooding him, building in his skull. Eyes massive and swollen, yet Jay can see everything surrounding him. But he can't make out any details among the liquescent vegetation.

He manages to close his eyes once more.

Doing this a lot, blacking out and waking up to more things gone to rot.

I'm beginning to prefer the nothingness.

It's comforting, in a way. Familiar too. Welcoming. Somewhere without worries. Cares. Just drift forever and not be bothered by anything ever.

A voice makes everything tremble. Overhead, gibberish speaks, but some becomes coherent:

"Got him."

"It."

"Retrieved."

Excitement in the heightening voice, a feeling Jay can't fathom.

"Done."

"Deal."

"Soon."

In the abyss, he rolls away from the words. Sinking, the void opens its gullet, and Jay lets it devour him once more.

The television is turned on high on the dresser against the peeling, yellow wall. Cowboys shoot guns; women hoot and scream; someone snarls. He's lying in the tub, head arched back against the drain, mouth open. Lights off. The taste of his station-issued Glock is like sucking an oiled pipe, the grease bitter on his tongue, the barrel digging into the roof of his mouth at an angle.

The way he lies there will mean minimal mess, easy clean-up for the poor soul in the morning. He doesn't want to cause any more hassle than he has to. The motel staff didn't do anything to him.

He's taken aback that there are no tears, no sobbing. Expected turnout from unexpected events, like shrugging when someone gets hurt from doing something stupid. What did you think was going to happen?

He closes his eyes.

Takes a deep breath and—

—Eyes open as gunpowder and flames burn his throat. Hacking the charred taste of flesh and smoke staining his tongue, Jay gasps for air, wrenched from the tub of the motel bathroom. Crews is at his side, urging him to lay back down on the bed, to settle. He looks the same as he did two days ago, as if Jay anticipated anything different. Patchy light brown beard, bald, bulbous nose, and wide-set, beady eyes.

A tube filled with yellow-green fluid runs from Jay's wrist to a silicone bag hanging from a peg on the wall on the renter's entry. Chairs and a table are folded against the wall. Five patches on his chest are plugged into a large box to his other side, an EKG but pink. His heart rate through the roof, the line zigzagging frantically. Other monitors that are entirely foreign to him show other information.

"Chill!" Crews shouts, standing, pushing Jay down. "You're fucking fine. Everything's okay."

Jay blinks back tears, white-knuckling the cot's sides. Finally catches the ever-fleeting air and gradually his lungs fill, settle. His heart follows. Crews steps back, meaty hands raised.

"Wh—what happened?" Jay says.

"You were basically dead is what happened." Crews sits back on his seat, hands on his lap. He's still wearing the same outfit as when he brought Jay on board: navy blue jumpsuit, top half down and arms tied around his round waist; white beater covering pudge, tufts of curling hair poking out the top.

"Felt like it," he says.

"So, you going to tell me what the hell happened? You were pretty fucked up when I got to you."

"Well..." Jay looks from Crews to his own body, realizing his wrists are strapped down by beige cuffs. Moves his ankles to discover the same... *No*—he has blackened fingers and toes, wispy spiraling tendrils unfurling under his nails. When he moves them they have a holographic sheen.

The captain...

"No," he says, facing Crews. Things click into place, a puzzle finally solved. Crews's hands aren't empty and on his lap anymore but holding a part of the yellow-green tube, his thumb on a button.

"What the fuck are you doing?" Jay jerks his limbs, grits his teeth, screams. "Let me go! Set me free, asshole. I did what you wanted me to do, I finished the dumb fucking job."

Crews says nothing as he presses the button. Warmth floods Jay as red-brown liquid surges into the tube. Heat crazily climbs his limbs and his neck, and as his face flashes with relaxing tides. He can't fight anymore and his eyes close.

Jay comes to slowly. Crews is still on the stool, holding the tube, lemon-lime again. They face each other and Jay immediately asks, "What are you doing to me? Where are we?"

"On the transporter. Don't remember if I showed you there was a cot or not." He lifts his flat hands, presenting it. "There it is. Anyway, we're cruising to an undisclosed location. Found out the AI on this thing isn't as shitty as I thought. Still terrible though."

"Why—why the straps?" He lifts his ankles and wrists half-heartedly.

"Don't want you to hurt yourself or me, really," he says, chuckling.

Jay glances over his toes and fingers. The webbing, rainbow-gleaning tendrils root past his nails now, curving under his skin, becoming faint, flowing teal veins.

"Hurt myself? Hurt you? Why would I want to do that?"

"Better question is why wouldn't you, in the shape that you are?"

He mouths, "What," then says, "Just tell me what's going on. Cut the bullshit."

"Fine, I'll be straight, only because I like you a little." He leans in, hairy forearms on his knees. "I needed a body to harbor the infection on the *Candlewood*. Had to be a HUSK though, not human, as you could tell with what happened to the cap. HUSKs don't have the faults we do with our immune system, our blood, our genetics. Comes in very handy when dealing with viruses and infections." He laughs, looks away, back. "Ever wonder why you didn't die all those times in there? That artificial shit has its upsides."

"Viruses? Infections? The captain was that thing—"

"All of the above. I didn't lie about owning the ship, bought it ages ago at an auction. But I did lie about not knowing what the hell was going on inside it. Knew all about it long before you were booted up. Thought for a bit we wouldn't need you, really; the cap might've worked out, but like I said before, flesh and bone ain't nothing compared to all the modified bullshit you're made from."

Jay's head throbs. His mind races, pushing against the interior of his skull. He wants to scream, wants to vomit out the incoherent words rampaging in his head, but the only thing that comes out is, "But..."

"Look Jay," he says. "I'll just answer all those questions bouncing in your head. This isn't my first stint, so I'll save us both a lot of time. I got word it was sent on the *Candlewood* some time ago, so that put everything into motion. The virus needs a place to incubate, like an egg, even after it's freed. Couldn't just drop it willy-nilly like some others work." Crews sighs, runs a hand over his scalp. "Like humans, it needs to feed off of stuff; needs a cozy, airtight place to fester and grow. Problem was by the time I knew about the cap, he was too far gone. Turned into that dog or whatever. So, I figured humans probably aren't the play and tried a HUSK—you—on the cheap instead."

"It transformed me," he says. "I *remember* my life—Nicole, Ashleigh, houses and places, my own *death*. I could... I could smell and taste things, I cried for fuck's sake... It *made* me human."

Crews sits back, crosses his arms over his breasts. "I'm going to be frank with you, Jay. You're as much human as that cot you're lying on is. Everything you remember is bullshit. Fake. Even your name isn't real. All the shit you recall was coded into you before you were powered on."

He scratches his chin. "Don't you think it's odd that you didn't remember most of that bull until *I* told you?"

"But my family, my senses... My *suicide*," he says, desperate, throat tight, "the way I did it—"

"Same thing. All HUSKs need a RFD before being brought online. Without one, it causes problems with the coding. Existential stuff. Your wife. Sister. Names. Job. Places. Your entire life before now was all written by some Gram'r in a hideaway smoke-den in Elusk. Didn't you also think it was weird you didn't remember anything about your job? Like actually doing it? Your captain, co-workers, police and investigation procedures?"

Despite not wanting to, his head shakes.

"Exactly. Who the fuck cares how all that worked back when? It didn't matter to the job at hand, and it costs more for detailed histories, so I told 'em to nix it. And to your whole weak bit about the virus making you human, that's a load of shit too. It's unpredictable, something found in a swamp on some random planet years ago. All we know about it is what it *can* do, what it potentially *could* do. So, taste, smell, and the waterworks. Yeah, great, you have those things. Feel better with them?"

Tears flood his eyes, and he searches for answers not there. His chest falls inward, hollow, his stomach an ever-consuming, ever-dropping maw. He inhales air he no longer wants through a strained throat. Murky sweat coats him. Jay doesn't know what to say, what to do, where to go. Everything he was, is, and will be is a lie; everything he believed to be fact, to be true about himself, is a fictional tale written by someone in front of a computer.

He isn't Jason, Jay. All that he thought to be true, what made him who he's now, is artificial. Every false memory of Nicole and Ashleigh speeds through his dwindling mind, a rapid montage of everything he loved and felt and lost. He never experienced the pain, not really, nor the agony and despair that drove him to end his own life.

Was I ever a person?

A person who lived, years and years ago?

Or is the foundation of my being fake too?

What's real or not?

Is this place even real?

Am I?

What's my purpose?

But the answer is there, unflinching, impossible to ignore no matter how much rumination he goes through: a pawn. Some piece in a larger game he couldn't have possibly known he was a player in.

Am I the first to have this happen?

The last?

Has Crews done this to other poor souls before?

"No," he whispers. *This is impossible. Absurd. It's all a lie.*

I just...

It can't...

No way it's...

But... it could *be.*

In the well of his circuitry, he simply doesn't and can't know. The seed of doubt planted grows quickly. Mind, memories, emotions, experiences. The world is upside down, but is he the one falling or has the world truly been flipped over? What is what and who is who?

He smiles.

Grimaces.

Shakes his head.

Nods.

He clenches and unclenches his hands as though pumping some sort of semblance of truth into his veins.

A sharp fissure shoots from the base of his neck to his forehead.

"Why me?" he spits.

"Honestly, Jay? You were the cheapest at the time, and I wasn't looking to spend most of my budget on fodder. Didn't need any of those bells and whistles fancier models come with." He grins, slaps Jay's leg. "And look, it turned out great. You got those features for free!"

"Was anything you said true?" *I can't be all data, ones and zeros. I have to be something* real. "About me?"

"You were a person, once, a long time ago."—*At least I got one answer*—"All HUSKs need a foundation to build upon, like a house. Can't grow a garden without soil. But besides that..." He scratches behind his ears. "No. Everything else was fake."

Jay remains silent, futilely attempting to process the hurricane of new information. Drowning in information and uncertainty, he reaches for solid ground only to have the undertow rip his feet down and cast his maddening mind asunder again.

Over and over he tries to make it make sense, make the shapes fit into the correct places, make the bomb Crews planted inside his head stop before it explodes. But he can't no matter which way he looks at it or which pieces seem likely to fit.

He wants to fight it. Beat it back. Stomp it into a hole it cannot escape from.

Wants to believe more than anything that the past fortifying his present is as real as he is now, but logic and rationale refuse to bend to his faith, his optimistic ideologies.

I'm a mannequin.

A robot.

Plastic and circuits and alloy and silicon and metal joints and—fuck.

A husk...

"Now what?"

"We wait until the infection reaches its peak," Crews say, "then drop you off."

"Then?"

"That's about it. The virus will do the rest."

"What the fuck's the point of any of this?" he shouts. "Why do you need me? Why do you *need* the virus?"

"You won't be around to remember it, so why the fuck not?" He laughs, his chest jiggling. "Rich folk need the ball to start rolling toward their goal, so they want to get it going by instilling terror into everyone with some horrifying disease. It's not just the poor saps who want humanity to return to the Motherland."

"Earth? Rich people want to go *back* to a dying planet? Can't they just... go there with their cash?"

"Some do, yeah." He nods. "But money doesn't solve everything, especially extremist views. They want a do-over. Not only the rich people, but *all people.* It's everything or nothing for them, and you know how powerful people are. They use the penniless masses to serve their needs." Leaning in, he whispers, "But you know what I really think Jay? I think they're lying to me, to everyone, about their so-called goal. I think those fuckers plan to force *only* those at the bottom of the social hierarchy from the Moon and Mars so they can have them both and Sola all to theirselves."

Crews reclines, resting his hands behind his head, revealing two tattoos, one on each arm—a hollow circle with a silhouette raindrop in the middle on the left; a circle filled in black, a raindrop above it on the right. He notices Jay noticing and says, "In the end, I don't give a flying shit what happens to who, because playing both sides ensures I always get paid, like I said before. I work for whoever has the most money."

I'm a...

"I'm a fucking explosive."

He nods.

"And you're a gutless piece of shit," he spits through the hot tears. "A shill. A whore. A two-timing, stupid, fat, selfish prick, and I hope this damn ship explodes and kills us both, because you don't deserve to live."

Crews laughs. "Don't get too pissed, Jay. It's not personal or anything. A man gotta eat."

"Fuck you."

Grabbing the yellow-green tube, he presses the button. Brown-red floods Jay's system and darkness consumes him.

Again, Jay's empty vision becomes awash by the waking world. There's something solid and hard beneath him. Cold, too. A few feet in front of him is green, and past that, murky blue. He blinks the haze away to find he's lying on the bench he sat on ages ago in the park. Green becomes fake grass; murky blue becomes the pond with film moving atop. False trees surround everything with cloth-like leaves.

His hands are almost entirely black save for the cerulean veins rooting up his forearms, furling into pulsing hexagons in his bicep, sending coolant through him. Frigid but hot. Liquid covers his face, but he can't see it against his charcoal flesh when wiped away. A cramp bolts from his abdomen to his chest, and his lungs flood with fire. Cinders smolder in his stomach, spitting coals into his groin and legs, becoming ice chips in his feet.

Doubling over, he holds his belly as he dry-retches into the grass. Realizes he's nude, but he can't focus on that—thumb tacks and nails push up his throat, poking through innards like paper. The pain gives enough reprieve for him to sit back, run his hand through hair to find no hair at all. Bald. Each fingertip on his scalp thunders.

"Can we go home soon?" a little boy says. Jay steals a glance while he walks with, presumably, his father. Both pale and share the same hazel eyes and blonde hair. They're holding hands as they enter from the right side of the park. "I'm getting tired."

The father laughs. "Soon, we're almost there." He points to the other side of the area, where one of the clustered, narrow buildings wait for their arrival.

Jay's veins bloom over the green-blue, shimmering with a metallic glint. Lava pours over the brim, widening, spilling. The cold-heat radiates from everywhere. Grass, pond, space and trees, his sigh turns monochrome. Charred fat prickles his tongue; burnt paper clogs his nose.

"Get moving, Jay," Crews chirps.

He slaps both ears. Empty.

"Don't bother looking for a comm, idiot. It's implanted into your head."

"I won't do it," Jay says. "I'm not going to infect all these people."

"Figured you'd say that."

Without consent, Jay rises from the bench and stumbles around it toward the boy and his father.

"There's more shit in you than you can imagine, Jay. You don't own that body, I do. HUSKs are something else, aren't they?"

Clenching his teeth, Jay attempts to dig his heels into the ground, to turn away, fall to his knees, do something to stop his course, but his body won't listen.

"Dad, what's that man doing?"

The father faces Jay. "What the hell—Why the fuck are you naked? Stop before you get hurt."

Veins push against flesh, beads and buds teem inside.

"Stop, asshole!" The man puts his son behind him. "Or I'll put you down, swear to God."

"Can't," he huffs out, "Stop."

His skin is peeling. Layer upon layer upon layer curls back, allowing something deeper and older to fill the delicately overlapping gold-speckled shells. Black-and-white turns completely blue that turns red to yellow to green to kaleidoscopic and holographic, and Jay can make out their outlines as they fray at the seams. Their oily innards and viscera viewable, their hearts delectable incubators for what's coming.

"What's happening to him, dad?" the boy says, beginning to cry. "What are those blue things in his eyes?"

The man puts up his fists. "I swear that if you come any closer, I'm going to knock you the fuck out."

Unheeded, Jay walks on. More people, more innocent vessels to carry the growth, come into the park. People are no longer just outlined but illuminated, showing not only the nitty-gritty of their anatomy but the world too. Trees, grass, water, cement, ground; buildings in the distance, the wall on the horizon. All of it will harbor the flora. Even the stars seem reachable.

"I can't," Jay laboriously says. "Can't. Stop. This. Ru—"

Mercury seeps from his gums, drills plunge into his teeth, and a fiery lump forces his throat to widen, making its way to his mouth.

The man strides toward him, teeth bared. "I warned you, jackass."

Jays arms open, muscles and sinew flaying from artificial bone. Hyperreal yellow and green vinery are disgorged like intestines. They hit the ground like fresh meat and curl, and before anyone can think, "What the hell is that?" they're darting at the man, his son, the bystanders. Quads and shins split down the center, regurgitating tendrils and saplings; his gut pukes three bouquets of crimson flowers; gold-beaded, gray roots ram through his chest, destroying his ribcage; every piece of what Jay eviscerated gives access to what he was always meant to be.

"Thanks for all your help, Jay," Crews says. "I really mean it."

Obese petals bloom from his torn mouth, a pallid stigma rising high above all, and blinds the audience with radiant, magnificent life.

Their screams are the last thing Jay hears before all turns black.

Acknowledgements

Thanks to the team at *Fedowar Press* for taking a chance with his book, and all the help they've provided making it the best it can be. I also want to thank all the editors I've worked with over the years, I wouldn't have gotten here without them.

Thanks to JT, JD, and the Kids. Even though I hardly show it, I always appreciate your support.

Thanks to the weird fiction/horror community for always being supportive of every writer, big or small. Special shout-outs to the folks on Twitter, the Books of Horror group, r/Weirdlit, the Tenebrous Press and Shortwave Publishing Discord servers, and the HWA Pittsburgh chapter. Unfortunately, I can't list everyone, but the people I've befriended over the years deserve their own mention (no particular order): Gwendolyn Kiste, Scott J. Moses, Kyle Winkler, Matt Wildasin, Robert Ottone, Sara Tantlinger, Katherine Silva, Michael Wehunt, David Peak, Alex Woodroe, Matt Blairstone, Alan Lastufka, Mike Davis, RJ Murray, Orrin Grey, Sam Richard, Joe Koch, Sarah Budd, Mindy Rose, Beth Djonne, Nick Roberts, Briana Morgan, Elford Alley, Emma Editrix, Matt Vaughn, and so many others.

About the Author

Micah Castle is a weird fiction and horror writer. His stories have appeared in various magazines, websites, and anthologies. He's the author of *Reconstructing a Relationship*, and *The World He Once Knew*.

While away from the keyboard, he enjoys spending time with his wife, playing with his animals, spending time in the woods, and can typically be found reading a book somewhere in his Pennsylvania home.

You can find him at his website: www.micahcastle.com, or on other platforms: www.linktr.ee/micahcastle.

CONTENT WARNING

Self-harm, suicide, suicide idealization, miscarriage.

If you or someone you know is in crisis, there are options available to help cope. You can call or text the 988 Suicide & Crisis Lifeline at any time to connect with a trained crisis counselor, or visit their website to chat with a trained crisis counselor at 988lifeline.org.

More from Fedowar Press

Bloodtooth by D.W. Hitz, a small-town coming of age horror compared to Needful Things crossed with A Nightmare on Elm Street with strong IT vibes:

After nightmares begin in the small town of Custer Falls, Montana, in 1992, it'll be thirty years before they end.

Available now from online bookstores or signed from Fedowar.com.

Uncanny Valley Days by C.J. Sampera

Rocked by grief and recurring apparitions of her dead brother, Olivia is losing her grip on reality and may have inadvertently invoked a cybernetic, serial-killing slasher demon. Or is it all in her head?

Available now from online bookstores.

The Frightful Tales of Louis & Lovely by Noelle Strommen

Louis and Lovely just moved into their new house. When they find a mysterious treehouse nearby with a new book waiting for them inside, they are unprepared for what awaits them.

When they start reading, and things go terrifyingly crazy, they want to restore the world around them and keep their family safe, they must survive the dark twists and turns of all six stories within the Frightful Tales.

Available now from online bookstores.

Dear Creator by Ast Geil

The apocalypse has come, and the Dear Creator is behind it. But what can humans really do in the face of godly injustice?

Available now from online bookstores.

Camp Slasher Lake: Volume One, winner of the 2023 Spatterpunk Award for Best Anthology.

A tribute to the glorious slasher movies of the 1980s, Volume 1.

Featuring stories from: John Adam Gosham, Gerri R. Gray, Patrick C. Harrison III, Carlton Herzog, D.W. Hitz, Derek Austin Johnson, J.D. Kellner, Brian McNatt, Nicholas Stella, & Vincent Wolfram

Available now from online bookstores or Fedowar.com.

Camp Slasher Lake: Volume Two

Another tribute to the glorious slasher movies of the 1980s, Volume 2.

Featuring stories from: Jay Bower, Justin Cawthorne, Kay Hanifen, D. W. Hitz, Brett Mitchell Kent, Aaron E. Lee, Kevin McHugh, Carl R. Moore, Daniel R. Robichaud, Darren Todd, & Mark Wheaton.

Available now from online bookstores or Fedowar.com.

Cody Was Here and Other Stories by D.W. Hitz

Cody Was Here and Other Stories is a chilling collection of works. They range from tales within Hitz's town of Custer Falls, known well from his novels and novellas, to stories of Sci-Fi Horror, Folk Horror, and even a ghost story.

Available now from online bookstores or Fedowar.com.

Gods are Born by D.W. Hitz

This is not the world you know. When aliens crashed on Earth, everything changed. Humanity has been decimated by predators and plague. Electromagnetic waves render most technology useless. The survivors are afflicted by strange mutations—some troubling, others amazing.

Gods are Born is a mature sci-fi read with elements of horror and graphic violence that follows the paths of seven extraordinary beings as they struggle to survive, find peace within themselves, and ultimately, defeat the King and something far worse than they can imagine.

Available now from online bookstores or Fedowar.com.

Thank you for reading.

9 781956 492491